LAST SONG FOR A RETURNING EXILE

George Lyttle

Last Song For A Returning Exile

All text copyright © of George Lyttle
Cover Design copyright © of George Lyttle
(Images courtesy of Vecteezy.com)

All rights reserved. No part of this book may be scanned, uploaded, reproduced, distributed or transmitted in any form or by any means whatsoever without written permission from the author, except in the case of brief quotations embodied in critical articles and reviews.

This is a work of fiction. Names, characters, business, events and incidents are the products of the author's imagination. Any resemblance to actual persons, living or dead, or actual events is purely coincidental.

First Published 2023
Printed in the UK

DEDICATION

For my family for their continued support and encouragement.

Thank you all for believing in me.

CHAPTER ONE
****

It was a normal Saturday afternoon in the crowded lounge of The Liberty Arms in the New Town Road area of the City of Drumfast. Glen McElroy and his cousin Brian Wharton breezed into the bar and took their usual seats over in the corner well away from the older patrons who were standing chattering at the bar counter as they attempted to put the world to rights. The two young men had just returned from watching their local soccer team Drumfast United losing once again to the local rivals Drumfast City. Glen was a slim seventeen year old who stood around five foot eleven in height. A shock of auburn hair framed his handsome face and it cascaded over the collar of his bomber jacket and nestled just past his neck. It was obvious his body had a lot of filling out to do before he reached full manhood.

'Two pints of lager Barney,' Glen ordered and the veteran barman smiled as he poured the drink from the pumps into two pint glasses.

'Stuffed again Glen,' he said. 'I don't know why you bother following that bad lot home and away. It won't get any better until they sack that manager McGuigan.'

Glen lifted the two pints and shook his head. 'I think he has only got another two matches to turn it around. If not, he is on his way up the road.'

'Maybe if you had stuck at it and trained harder you could have been signed by them. You were certainly good enough,' added the barman.

'I think the Printers League is just about my standard now Barney,' laughed Glen as he moved over to where his cousin was sitting.

A smile encompassed Barney's plump, highly coloured face and he laughed into himself as he watched the young man walking over to join his cousin. He had a lot of time for young Glen but the same could not be said for Brian Wharton. The barman thought this particular teenager was shady in the extreme and seemed to be in the company of dubious elements when Glen was at work during the week at the local printing works. Wharton never seemed to hold down a job for any length of time but mysteriously was never short of money even though his apparent main form of income was from unemployment relief.

Brian Wharton was much the same slim build as Glen but his features were a good deal plainer and were framed by long black hair which also hung over the collar of his jacket. He had an ongoing battle with acne on his thin, pale face which meant he did not stand out in a crowd. At times he resented his cousin's popularity in the bar especially with Barney the barman, but most of all he envied Glen's attachment to his girlfriend Marlene. When they were younger and starting to discover the attraction towards the opposite sex they had both vied for her attention. Unluckily for him she had set her cap on Glen and he had to watch from the sidelines as the pair grew ever closer together.

After setting the pints of lager on the table Glen removed his jacket, hung it over the back of the chair and pulled the replica Drumfast United football shirt down to straighten it over his jeans. His cousin did likewise but flung his jacket on a bench seat nearby.

'I'm off for a waz in the toilet,' announced Glen as he took a first sip of the lager and stood up to his five foot eleven height.

'Make sure you wash your hands afterwards,' joked Brian as he watched his cousin disappear into the mens' washroom.

Looking around the bar to ensure that Barney was busy serving customers and he was not being watched he slipped his hand into the pocket of his jeans and pulled out three small paper packets each containing an amount of white powder. These were wraps of cocaine which were the remains of a lot he was supposed to sell for the drugs organisation he was working for as a dealer most days of the week. He had frittered away the money he owed these people for the sale of the drugs he had been supplied with. All week he had been trying to think of a way to extract himself from the imminent danger he was in when it was discovered that he had frittered away the organisation's money.

Wharton looked over at Glen's jacket hanging on the back of the chair opposite and the solution to his problem was staring him straight in the face. If he lied that the drugs were stolen from him there was a slim chance he might get out of this situation in one piece. He slid over the nearby bench seat towards the opposite jacket and slipped the three wraps into Glen's inside pocket before moving back to his previous position. He quickly took up a relaxed frame sipping casually from his pint glass as Glen returned to the table.

'Relief beyond belief,' laughed Glen as he sat down and drank from the pint glass completely unaware of the wraps of narcotics in the inside pocket of his bomber jacket.

'I'll get us another couple of pints,' offered Brian Wharton hoping to keep his cousin in the bar for at least another half an hour.

'I've only drank half of this one,' countered Glen. 'I have to meet Marlene at half past seven to go to the cinema. Get me a half and I'll pour it into this one.'

'Rightho. You can't keep the blessed Marlene waiting,' joked Wharton half sarcastically as he made his way to the bar counter. He pushed his way through the standing patrons and ordered a pint and a half of lager from the unsmiling Barney who took the money without exchanging a word with the young man. Obviously there was an extreme dislike in both cases.

Brian sat the glasses down trying to act so casual as if nothing had transpired when Glen had gone to the toilet. He engineered the conversation towards the match that afternoon and as usual thinking he could spot the defects on their beloved team.

'There is no spine in the team,' he said. 'We need a good centre back, a box to box midfielder and a big centre forward who can head a ball into the net and not over the bar like that twat we have now.'

Glen smiled and was just about to add to the conversation when the door of the bar opened and in walked Greg Bennet and his associate Eddie McGaughey. These were two men who were not to be trifled with. They were not at the top of the local drug organisation but seemed to hold more sway there than their positions deemed possible. They were the enforcers and it was rumoured that Bennet knew too much about the operations of the leaders of the organisation. The rumour had it that he had lodged incriminating documents with his solicitor in case anything happened to him should there be a fallout and he fell out of favour with the top men in the organisation. The papers would be released in the event of his death thereby making him virtually untouchable in the gang during his life time.

Bennet was a stocky individual who stood around five feet eight inches in height. His features had not seen a razor blade in quite a few days. He preferred the unshaven look as it covered most of his pock marked face and along with his close cut gelled black hair and dark expensive clothing this had the appearance of giving him an air of menace. His companion McGaughey had a somewhat chequered past and had just been released from prison after doing a stretch for demanding money with menaces. He was also a heavily built individual whose lived-in face looked square in shape.

It was evident he did not dress as elegantly as his boss preferring to wear a denim jacket and jeans which he thought also gave him an air of menace with long dirty blonde hair cascading over the side of his face and along the collar of his jacket. McGaughey walked with a slight limp emanating from his younger days when a bullet was inserted into his kneecap for anti social behaviour around the district.

The men standing at the bar stopped talking and kept their heads down as the pair looked around and spied the two young men sitting at the table in the corner of the lounge. They walked over and stood seemingly towering above the lads. Brian Wharton's face was etched with fear while Glen just sat and waited to hear what the two men had to say to his cousin. After all he had never any dealings with Bennet and McGaughey in the past so any business they were about to discuss was with his cousin.

'Right Wharty where's my cash?' demanded Bennet. 'You've had all week to hand it over along with any unsold wraps.'

'Look Greg I don't have it,' replied Wharton. 'The money and the stuff was in my jacket pocket last Saturday after the match here in the bar but when I got home it was missing.'

'A likely story,' said McGaughey. 'And where did the wraps mysteriously disappear to? Into thin air I suppose.'

Glen looked over at his cousin and his relaxed mood was starting to disappear as he had been with Brian Wharton in the bar that same Saturday. He had been unaware and was now alarmed that Brian had been carrying drugs in his denim jacket, especially to a football match. There was a chance that they could have been frisked on entry to the ground for bottles or missiles which could be hurled at opposing supporters during exchanges during the game.

'Check his jacket and the other lad's jacket as well,' ordered Bennet to his sidekick.

'Wow, hold on a minute,' shouted the now angry Glen as he stood up to block McGaughey's access to his jacket. 'Whatever has been going on between Brian and you has nothing to do with me.'

'We'll see about that,' said Bennet as McGaughey pushed Glen back into his seat and grabbed the jacket from the back of the chair.

At first McGaughey searched Brian Wharton's jacket and nothing was uncovered. He then handed Glen's jacket to Bennet who searched the two outside pockets and threw a set of door keys and a packet of chewing gum on to the table almost knocking a pint of lager over. When he slipped his hand into the inside pocket he pulled out the three wraps this time placing them in his own pocket so that nobody in the bar could see them.

'Right you two into the office at the back of the bar,' ordered Bennet as he wanted an investigation far away from any prying eyes from the patrons at the bar counter.

It was a well known rumour that the Liberty Arms was part or even fully owned by the drugs cartel. Hence Greg Bennet was able to organise operations from the sanctuary of this office at the rear of the bar. Bennet stepped in behind a wooden desk sat down and ordered McGaughey to push the two young men into a couple of chairs in front of him.

'Look Greg I don't know how Glen got hold of the stuff,' Wharton starting blubbing, 'all I can think of is when I went the bogs last Saturday it was taken from my pocket. He probably needs the money from a deal to take his girlfriend out on a date.'

The red mist gathered over Glen's eyes and he made a dive for his deceitful cousin only to be held back in a crushing arm embrace by the powerful Eddie McGaughey.

'You lying toe rag Brian,' he spewed. 'If I get free from this gorilla I'll tear you apart.'

'You'll tear nobody apart,' said Bennet. 'You know what happens to anybody who disrespects the organisation. I have a lot of respect for your father since we went to school together so I will forego a kneecapping this time.'

'You know my old man would knock your lights out if you ordered this,' replied Glen. 'He's not afraid of you or any of the scum that peddles this stuff around the district.'

'He might be scared of the people further up the chain when they hear his son has been operating a little scheme independent of them,' said Bennet. 'I hear he's overseas working at the moment so he is in for a shock when he gets back and finds you gone out of the city.'

'What do you mean out of the city?' asked Glen whose anger was once again welling up.

'I'm being lenient on you.' replied Bennet. 'The usual for this is kneecapping but I'm letting you get out of the city with your legs intact.'

'That's so really kind of you,' said Glen sarcastically. 'Seeing I had nothing to do with this. Look no further than that lying twat sitting over there.'

Brian Wharton dropped his head and stayed silent. He knew he had probably extradited himself out of a very sticky situation at the expense of his cousin. Since their schooldays he had always lived in Glen's shadow. His untrustworthiness and in the popularity stakes with their mates but most importantly with the opposite sex meant he was second best in both areas. Although the two followed their favourite team together there was always envy in his mind when his cousin stepped out with the pretty Marlene. When he made a play for her on a number of occasions she had knocked him back in no uncertain terms. This was pay back time.

'Wharty get out of here, I'll speak to you later,' commanded Bennet. 'Be back here at seven. I'll have another lot for you to offload and this time keep it safe or you'll get the same as this numpty here.'

Wharton didn't need a second invitation and almost leaped off the chair to get out of the office before there was any further punishment forthcoming either from Bennet, McGaughey or indeed Glen McElroy. If his cousin should decide to catch up with him before his exile from the city he was going to stay well out of his way. He intended to keep a low profile even to stay away from his home until that evening when he was due to report back to The Liberty Arms.

'Get up to your house and pick up any belongings you need,' said Bennet to Glen. 'Say your goodbyes and be on the next train to wherever you intend to live and don't come back until I say so. Now get out of here before I change my mind.'

Glen rose up and glared at the two men before imparting a final shot at the both of them. 'Looks like you both are not blessed with the intelligence to be detectives. You know fine well I have not been peddling this rubbish but it looks like Brian is one of your top dealers so he is getting a bye ball in this case. When my Da gets back he will be down to see you.'

'Is that a threat you cheeky young twat?' interjected Eddie McGaughey. 'Your old man may think he is a tough guy but he knows better that to tangle with the men at the top of this team.'

'Yeah you bet he knows better,' laughed Bennet. 'Now get out and don't show your face around here again until we give you the go-ahead to return.'

'I'll be returning all right,' said Glen, 'but when I do there'll be a lot of old scores to be settled make no mistake about that.'

'Just get out before Eddie gives you a fat lip,' threatened Bennet.

Glen was tempted to throw another insult towards the two men but resisted as it would only throw fuel onto the fire. He slammed the office door shut and as he passed by the bar counter he gave a quick wave to Barney who was busy drying glasses with a white tea towel. The barman guessed that the meeting in the back office had not gone well as Glen had always plenty of time to talk to him. How he wished that The Liberty Arms would return to the respectable establishment it had been just over a year ago before the owner then was forced to sell to the drugs organisation.

A lot of the older clientele had drifted away and now frequented the bars further up the road. It was a sign of the times in the district and not a good one at that as people like Bennet and McGaughey seemed to rule the roost spreading fear in old and young alike. Barney had thought if he had been able to get bar work somewhere else he would be off like a flash. However, jobs were at a premium in the city as even good carpenters like Glen's dad were forced to find work fitting out palaces and super yachts in the middle east far away from their home and loved ones.

CHAPTER TWO
****

He walked slowly towards his house situated in a private housing estate on the outskirts of the city. Glen was trying to think how he could explain what had happened in the bar to his mother who would be living on her own when he would be forced to leave the city. His father's contract in the middle east still had another two weeks to run so the only faint hope was that her sister Sarah, who was Brian Wharton's mother, might help to keep an eye on her in the meantime.

Glen had an up and down relationship with his aunt. She was a hard woman to get along with and had been divorced from Brian's father for over seven years. In Glen's mind his uncle's miss was his mercy as he had been living in a miserable marriage with this harridan of a woman. Her son could do no wrong in her eyes and he was able to manipulate her feelings which had resulted in the degenerate lifestyle he was able to pursue with impunity. His aunt's presence to look in on his mother was the best he could hope for until his father's return in a couple of weeks time. At least he would not be there to be in his aunt's presence should she be at the house on a regular basis in the interim.

As Glen reached his home he stood outside the front door for a few moments thinking how he was going break the news of his imminent departure from the city to his mother and eventually to his girlfriend Marlene. There was no way he was going to be able to sugar coat the news he was going to impart to his parent so he entered the kitchen where Anna, his mother, was preparing an evening meal for the both of them.

'You're cutting it a bit fine,' she announced as he appeared at the kitchen door. 'By the time you eat this and get ready to meet Marlene it will mean you'll miss the start of the film. Get this into you. Have a quick wash and rush down to her street to meet her.'

'Mum, I'm not going to be able to meet her tonight,' he sighed, his mind going into overdrive how he was going to break the information that would break his mother's heart in two.

'Don't tell me you are going back down to that Liberty Arms to drink again with that Brian,' she demanded. 'He is a bad influence on you and I worry he will get you into trouble someday.'

'Brian has got me into trouble all right,' replied Glen sadly. 'He has set me up in a tangle with Greg Bennet and Eddie McGaughey by planting three wraps of coke in my jacket pocket to get himself off the hook. Apparently he has been pocketing the money from the deals over the past few weeks and came up with a cock and bull story that they had been stolen. So when the wraps were found in my jacket they have assumed that I nicked the stuff and spent the money.'

Anna sat down on a kitchen chair and placed both hands over her bowed face. It was times like this that she wished her husband Derek was here to sort out this mess. She was a good looking woman who had kept herself in trim condition over the years but at this moment in time the worry of her son's predicament had placed years on her face as her frame sat slumped at the kitchen table.

'Surely they are not so stupid to believe Brian Wharton's story,' she cried. 'You have never been involved with these people, have you?'

'Mum you know I have given them a wide berth,' Glen replied. 'I earn enough dough from working overtime in my job to steer clear of that rubbish. All I ever wanted to do is have a couple of pints after the match on a Saturday and take Marlene out a few nights in the week.'

'I wish your Dad was here. He would be able to go down there and clear this up right away,' said Anna. 'What have you to do now? Are they demanding money from you to pay for the drugs?'

'Money wasn't mentioned. They want me out of the city right away to set an example to any of their dealers what would happen if they crossed them,' said Glen as he sat down on a chair beside his mother.

'How long for?' asked his mother.

'Indefinitely!' he replied.

The tears started to run down Glen's mother's face. He felt powerless as she sobbed and held on to both his hands tightly as if to never let them go. As he sat and looked at the state of his mother he swore that if he ever got his hands on his cousin he would tear him apart limb from limb.

Anna composed herself and worked out the next moves for her son. Her brother Andrew lived in the Govan district of Glasgow and he always had a soft spot for Glen and had hosted her husband and son in his flat when they travelled there for a football match. He was a confirmed bachelor so he would have the room to let his nephew stay there until things were sorted out in Drumfast once her husband Derek arrived back from working overseas.

'I'll go up and pack you some clothes and deodorants to see you through the next couple of weeks,' she said. 'Look out your razor, I don't want you looking like a tramp there.'

Glen smiled as his mother disappeared up the stairs to organise his travelling bag. His face suddenly dropped into a frown as he thought how word was going to be sent to Marlene as only a few houses in that working class district had in-house telephones. It looked like his mother would have to be the bearer of this shattering news to his girlfriend. Another dread struck him as thoughts were whirring through his mind. Would Marlene wait for him until he was allowed to return to Drumfast? There was plenty of lads who had their eye on her especially his deceitful cousin Brian who had been living in the hope that one day she would go out with him.

This Saturday had started out so brightly but now had turned out to be an extreme disaster. He went to the kitchen cabinet and lifted out his electric razor and waited for his mother to descend the stairs with his overnight bag. Anna entered the kitchen, placed the bag on the table and sat down once again looking sadly into her son's face without saying a word.

Glen broke the silence knowing what he was going to ask his mother would put additional pressure on her to what was already there. 'Mum there is no way I can get to Marlene to let her know what has happened. Will you tell her what has happened and assure her I am innocent?'

'Of course I will,' replied his mother. 'The thing I am dreading is telling your Aunt Sarah about this. She will be gloating and thinking that her Brian has steered well away from drugs unlike you.'

'She has never liked me anyway,' said Glen, 'but Mum, keep your thoughts to yourself. You will need her to look in with you until Dad gets back.'

'It's going to be hard,' replied Anna. 'Just as long as that Brian stays clear of this house I will mange it for the next couple of weeks.'

Glen kissed her on the forehead and went outside to walk to the corner of the street to enter the telephone box and order a taxi that would take him to the railway station. As he walked back up the street he looked at the rows of semi detached houses and thought how he was going to miss the comfort of the lifestyle that his hard working parents had provided for him.

They were happy with their own standard of living but his aunt was always in a facile competition with them as who had the superior home and who would be the most successful of the two cousins. His parents could never understand her attitude but as she was Anna's sister they gave her a bye ball to maintain peace in the family.

When he arrived back at the house his mother had her coat on ready to escort him to the taxi when it would eventually arrive. She decided to go to the phone box to inform her brother Andy that he was going to have a visitor for the foreseeable future. After that she would have to walk down to the New Town Road to the home of Marlene and inform the girl of the happenings of the day. This was something she was dreading as Glen was the only steady boyfriend that Marlene had ever been out with.

The taxi duly arrived ten minutes later and pulled up outside the house. Glen and Anna embraced and he tried to reassure her that he would be fine in Glasgow with his uncle.

'Mum don't let Sarah tell you otherwise,' he said forcefully. 'I was not dealing drugs. She can see no wrong in Brian but the truth will hopefully come out in the long run.'

He kissed her on the cheek once again and hopped into the back of the cab placing his bag on the seat beside him. Anna watched as the taxi motored down the street and turned the corner towards the city centre and the railway station. She wondered when she would ever see her son again in Drumfast. The only way they could meet up would be in Glasgow on the infrequent occasions that finance would allow.

Her only hope was that her husband could sort something out when he arrived home from working abroad. But that was a faint hope as she knew these people in the organisation had an unforgiving nature and even Derek, who could hold his own in a one to one scrap, would be powerless to take on the might of a whole cartel. It looked like their son would have to live in exile for ever unless something unexpected happened in the future.

Anna decided to wait until Derek arrived back from working in the middle east to let him know what had happened to Glen in his absence. He had only a couple of weeks left in his contract there so she thought it advisable to let him see it through. What his reaction would be when he found out what had happened was something she was not looking forward to.

CHAPTER THREE
****

Derek McElroy jumped out of the taxi, grabbed his suitcase and quickly walked round to the driver's side of the taxi which had transported him from the airport. He put his hand into his trouser pocket and pulled out a wad of notes before speaking into the open cab window to the driver.

'What's the damage mate?' he asked.

'We'll call it twenty quid,' the cabbie replied.

Derek extracted a twenty pound note and added a ten pound note as a tip for the driver. The man grinned with delight for the generous gesture and gave his benefactor a cheery wave before driving off down the street towards Drumfast city centre to pick up another fare.

As he lifted his case off the ground Derek looked up at his house and breathed a sigh of relief to be back in the bosom of his family. In addition to the cash he had a very valuable cheque in his pocket which he earned working in the middle east as a self-employed carpenter in the palaces and super yachts of the mega rich Arab princes.

He was so pleased with himself as he opened the front door and bellowed out a greeting that he was indeed home to resume his family life.

'Yo ho ho,' he yelled out. 'The traveller has returned.'

Derek was expecting his wife and possibly his son to come rushing into the hallway to greet him but the only person appearing was Anna who appeared downcast in the extreme. He looked completely confused when he looked at the pained expression on her face but tried to lighten things up by making a wisecrack.

'Maybe I should have stayed away for another couple of weeks as it looks like I have not been missed,' he laughed.

'Derek I'm so glad that you are back,' said Anna. 'Come into the living room and take a seat to hear what I have to tell you. You'll need to sit down when you find out what has happened.'

The pair sat down on the settee and Anna described the events which had happened the previous fortnight. With each sentence she could see Derek's blood starting to boil up. In his younger days he was a formidable opponent if anyone crossed him and he knew he had the measure of Greg Bennet and Eddie McGaughey in previous altercations when they pushed their luck with him in The Liberty Arms. There was no way he was letting this drop until he went to see the pair of them and attempt to sort out the situation his son had found himself in.

'As soon as I finish this cup of tea I'm hailing a taxi and going down to The Liberty Arms to find out what these two galoots have to say,' he announced. 'There's something fishy about this. I was never ever happy with our Glen going to the football matches and socialising with Brian Wharton. That boy is on the road to nowhere if you ask me.'

'Derek just be careful,' said Anna. 'It's not only them you have to deal with but that organisation that will back them to the hilt.'

'I'll be careful all right,' he replied. 'I'll be careful to knock the pair of their heads together if I don't get the right answers.'

Derek rose and went upstairs to have a quick wash and change the clothes he had been wearing on the flight from the middle east. As he bounded down the stairs Anna was waiting at the bottom to once again urge him to keep his hair-trigger temper under control once he reached The Liberty Arms. He kissed her and assured his worried wife that he would maintain self control and just put across his opinion in a forceful manner.

He waited, not very patiently, at the phone box which was situated farther down the street from his house. After striding back and forth outside the box for fifteen minutes the taxi eventually arrived and he asked the cabbie to take him to The Liberty Arms on the New Town Road. When the taxi drew up outside the hostelry he proffered a twenty pound note and waved away the offer of his change from the driver.

It had been a long time since Derek had entered the doors of The Liberty Arms and it would have been an even further distance of time had it not been the prevailing circumstances surrounding his son. Barney, the bar tender, looked up as the door swung open but was not completely surprised to see his old friend Derek McElroy enter the lounge.

'Good to see you again Derek,' he said greeting the big man as they shook hands. 'I heard you were coming back from overseas and I was half expecting you to find out what happened here.'

'Too right. I'm expecting answers Barney,' replied Derek. 'Are Batman and Robin in their hidey-hole at the back there?'

'Yes. They'll not be too happy to see you Derek but don't believe anything they say about young Glen and the drugs.' advised Barney.

'I won't,' replied Derek and he stormed away towards the back of the lounge where the office was situated.

Without knocking he pushed the door wide open very forcibly almost propelling Eddie McGaughey off his seat which was situated just behind it. McGaughey gathered himself together and moved over well out of way in case some punches were about to be delivered. Derek ignored him and stared straight at Greg Bennet as he sat behind the desk with a glass of whiskey in his hand.

'Good to see you back Derek,' Bennet lied. 'Can I offer you a drink?'

'I only drink with people I like,' replied Derek. 'I'm only here to find out what happened here to have my lad forced away from his family.'

Bennet sat for some seconds and pondered over what he was about to say to the increasingly angry Derek McElroy towering over him at the other side of his desk. He knew he would have to be extremely careful what he said due to previous violent situations with Glen's father. If he said the wrong thing the desk could end up on top of him. Derek, for his part, knew he would have to keep cool if progress, if any, was to be made. He waited to hear what Bennet was going to say.

'Derek, your boy was found bang to rights with three wraps of coke in his jacket,' Bennet started to explain. 'It looks like he was hoping to start up in business on his own with our merchandise.'

'For goodness sake, do you take me for a complete fool,' stormed Derek who was getting angrier on listening to the last statement. 'Glen has never dabbled in the dirt that you peddle. Look no further than his shifty cousin Brian. I want this exclusion lifted right away or I go to the law.'

'That would not be advisable,' said Bennet in a menacing tone. 'This has now gone well above my head. My superiors know what your attitude would be and they have a network of contacts in Glasgow They already know that your boy is staying with his uncle in the Govan area.'

At that moment Derek was tempted to land the desk on top of the man sitting on the other side and drop Eddie McGaughey with his fist into the bargain. Good sense prevailed and at that moment he realised that appealing to Bennet's better nature was useless.

'You haven't heard the last of this,' he warned as he opened the office door to leave. 'Sooner or later I will sort this out and Glen will return to help me do it.'

'Derek, this is business. Nothing personal as we all have to make a living and answer to those above us,' said Bennet.

'You mean a dirty business and your means of living only gives certain death to those poor idiots you trap into your web.' With that final remark Derek slammed the door and marched quickly past the bar counter giving a quick wave at Barney who was serving a customer.

He decided to walk home as the indigestion which had been troubling him over the past number of months flared up again. In the middle east he had regular bouts of heartburn and trapped wind but contented himself that this might be due the different dietary options in that part of the world. At times it had abated as he concentrated on his work and he had once again resumed composing song lyrics in the rest periods after a hard days work. This was a hobby going back from his younger days in years past.

On the way back home he pondered over the implied threat Bennet had made regarding him going to the law. He knew these people had tentacles spreading all over Europe and the city of Glasgow, in those terms, was only a stones throw away from Drumfast. It was more important at this moment in time that his son was safe.

When he arrived home Anna was in the kitchen preparing a late lunch. She immediately stopped to hear what had transpired at The Liberty Arms.

'Did you make any headway with Bennet?' she asked.

'Not really,' he sighed. 'It appears that they might know where Glen is staying in Glasgow and if I go to the police his life could be put in danger. They have contacts everywhere. I feel powerless to help my boy as two fists can't beat these people who are in the shadows everywhere.'

'I was just thinking when you left to go to see Bennet that it might be a good thing that Glen is out of the way at the moment,' said Anna. 'He might be better away from the atmosphere of drugs that's growing around this place, especially with his cousin in so deep. It could be too much of a temptation for him to get involved with the amount of money that's floating around the place.'

'Maybe you are right,' Derek replied. 'But the fact remains he is losing time with his family. It looks like we are between a rock and a hard place. We'll let Glen settle in Glasgow for now and see what transpires in the coming months. Andy will look after him well enough in the meantime.'

As Derek started his lunch and finished off a cheese sandwich the bloated feeling once again came over him and he felt really full even after this very light meal. Anna immediately noticed his discomfort and scolded him for not taking the Lansoprazole tablets the doctor had proscribed for the bouts of acid which had afflicted him before he had left to work oversees.

'If this keeps up you are going to make an appointment to see the doctor.' she advised.

'It'll settle down once these tablets start working again,' he replied.

'You know you should be taking them around half an hour before eating,' she once again scolded him.

'If it keeps up I'll go to see him, maybe next week,' Derek assured her hoping that remark would keep the peace.

However, weeks and months went by without Derek undertaking his promise to Anna to see the physician. Over that time he hid the extent of his discomfort by taking the tablets and keeping out of the way of his wife when bouts of trapped wind and forced burping occurred. As a self employed tradesman he was forced to continue working even though he was in pain at times. His strong constitution seemed to be enough to see him through the periods of pain.

Glen had settled well in Glasgow and his youthful Uncle Andy had become a firm friend. In the first eighteen months his parents made frequent trips to visit and the three men were able to take in football matches while Anna went on shopping expeditions in the city centre. No mention was ever made of Derek's condition and once again he journeyed on as if nothing was wrong.

Marlene had been writing regularly at first but he noticed in the past year and a half the messages had become few and far between. Maybe his fear that the distance between them was too great an obstacle for their relationship to flourish even further. If he had known of his father's deteriorating health this would be an added burden but it was kept a secret to him.

The pain in his stomach was getting worse and eventually Anna made an appointment to see the doctor behind her husband's back. Derek was forced to make the trip to the surgery where the doctor berated him for not coming to see him many months before. After an in-depth examination the doctor decided that a trip to hospital was in order to undertake a scan to discover the reason for the symptoms that Derek was having to live with.

A number of weeks went by until a letter arrived from the doctor's surgery to inform them that an appointment had been made for Derek to see the doctor as soon as possible. The physician's grim face told them that the result of a scan and a further biopsy did not hold out a positive outcome.

'The results of the scan have come back to me and I'm afraid it is not what I had hoped for,' he started off. 'It shows that the pain and discomfort in your stomach is due to a malignant tumour.'

'Oh no!' cried Anna as her head sank into her hands.

Derek grabbed her hand in an attempt to comfort her as she burst out crying and he went into pragmatic mode even though he was equally shaken by the result of the scan.

'What's the next stage doctor?' he asked. 'Is this thing treatable?'

'You can possibly have another twelve months if you keep to the regime that is led down for you,' the doctor replied. 'But, I am sorry to say the cancer is in an advanced stage and at first we can treat it with pain relief but eventually this disease will take you off your feet.'

'I'm self employed so I need to work to make a living,' Derek protested as the gravity of the situation he was in struck him like hammer blow.

Anna eventually composed herself as she could see her husband was becoming as equally distressed as herself. She spoke to him softly trying to reassure him of their financial position.

'Derek we have put quite a lot of money away over the past couple of years,' she said. 'Also Glen has been sending money every month and although I have been putting it away for him I know he would want us to use it for ourselves if things got tight.'

'Let me know if there is anything you need,' said the doctor as the pair left the surgery.

'Thanks doctor, we will,' replied Anna and they walked out of the building and on to the New Town Road to hail a taxi to take them back to the comfort of their home.

As predicted Derek's condition deteriorated over the next eleven months. He was forced to give up work and spent most of the day either resting on the settee or staying in bed for long periods. His final examination at the hospital informed him of the condition of his cancer that he was dreading. He had possibly only three weeks to live.

CHAPTER FOUR
****

Just over three years had passed by in his time in Glasgow. They seemed to have passed very quickly and Glen was now a strapping twenty-one year old. His employers at the printing company in Drumfast had thankfully passed over his particulars to their associate firm in Govan and that enabled him to finish his apprenticeship as a compositor there.

Over the intervening years frequent visits from his parents made the exile bearable and he engaged in a busy lifestyle working out at a local gymnasium and attending football matches with his good friend and uncle Andy. He was able to engage in a few liaisons with the opposite sex but these were usually short lived as his heart was still set on someday resuming his relationship with Marlene once again.

Little did he know that Brian Wharton had been spreading poison in her ear over the period of his absence regarding his supposed drug dealing and his lifestyle in Glasgow. His cousin had wormed his way into her affections and they were now an item much to the satisfaction of Brian's mother Sarah. This was the one time her son had come out on top on the supposedly ongoing competition with her nephew Glen.

Just as he was coming to terms with the news that his girlfriend had deserted him his mother had phoned a few weeks afterwards with the earth shattering news that his father had been diagnosed with inoperable stomach cancer. Glen had wondered why their visits had been less frequent over the previous three months although Derek's failing health was never mentioned on those occasions. He had noticed that his father seemed to have lost some weight but thought he had cut down his diet of fatty foods and had reduced his alcohol intake which was minimal in any case. It was then revealed that his dad had been attending hospital to have scans and biopsies taken and the tumour was diagnosed as malignant.

As he relaxed in his room after work one night his Uncle Andy knocked on the door and told him that his mother was on the phone and wanted to speak to him urgently.

'Your mother sounded as if she was ready to break down son,' said his uncle. 'Try to calm her down and make some sense on what she is trying to say.'

Glen rushed out of the room and grabbed the telephone which was sitting on the wrought iron table in the hallway of the flat.

'Hello Mum,' he said, 'Uncle Andy says you are in a bit of a state. What's wrong? Is dad all right?'

'No Glen he is not all right,' she replied. 'We were at the hospital today for his regular examination and when your father asked for the prognosis of the cancer he was told that he would be lucky to have three weeks left.'

'Do you mean he is going to die?' said the shocked Glen.

'That's what it means,' sobbed his mother.

'I'm coming back immediately,' declared Glen. 'I'll take my holidays early and the boss should okay it under the circumstances.'

'Glen you know that is not possible,' said his mother. 'Bennet still has a contract out on you if you set foot in Drumfast without his say so.'

'Sod Bennet,' shouted an enraged Glen. I'm going home no matter what he or that idiot McGaughey say.'

There was silence on the other end of the line and he wondered if his mother had fainted but the voice returned after what seemed like an eternity.

'There may be a another way round this,' said Anna. 'Under the circumstances Bennet may see reason. He always had a grudging respect for your dad since their school days although they had their beefs and gone on different paths over the years.'

'How can you get round this?' asked Glen. 'No matter what, I'm heading home as soon as I can.'

'Just hold on Glen,' argued his mother. 'I will go and see Bennet to persuade him to let you come back for a couple of weeks to be with your dad. A lot of water has flowed under the bridge these past three years so he may relent and you can come home without any hassles.'

'OK Mum, go and see him but no matter what he says I'm going home,' asserted Glen. 'Let me know tomorrow, but be sure of one thing, my bags will be packed ready to go.'

'Just be calm son,' said Anna, 'I'll ring you tomorrow evening when you get back from work.'

'Rightho, love you, tell Dad I was asking about him.' said Glen and he sat the phone down. Without saying anything to his uncle he went to his room and starting packing an overnight travelling case.

The next morning in Drumfast Anna waited impatiently until lunchtime would arrive when she would be sure that Greg Bennet would be in the office at the rear of The Liberty Arms. Although, in the past, her sister Sarah was not the most popular person in the McElroy household she had been most supportive since Derek's illness. Sarah indicated that she would stay in case Derek, who now spent most days in bed, would need anything while Glen's mother travelled to see Bennet at the bar.

Anna decided to walk the distance to the New Town Road which would give her the time to formulate what she was going to say to Greg Bennet. When she reached The Liberty Arms she stood outside for a moment to compose herself before entering the establishment.

Barney, the little portly barman, was lifting chairs down from the tables and placing them in position to prepare for the business of the day. He looked around when the door opened and the slim unfamiliar figure of Anna McElroy stood at the entrance still hesitating at first to come fully into the bar.

'My goodness Anna it's not often we see you around here,' he said in mock amazement. 'What brings you down to this neck of the woods?'

'I'm here to see Bennet to try to persuade him to allow Glen to come home to spend the last few weeks with his dad,' she said trying hard not to let the pent up emotions get the better of her.

'I was so sorry to hear about Derek,' replied Barney. 'I certainly missed him and Freddie Jenkinson when they decided to drink elsewhere, though I didn't blame them.' he added.

'Derek is not in a very good place at the moment,' said Anna. 'Although they are keeping him comfortable at the moment they may have to up the medication very soon to keep the pain at bay.'

Barney came closer to Anna and whispered in her ear. 'Why do these things happen to the good guys like your husband while scum like Bennet and McGaughey walk the streets safe and sound and healthy? It's a crying shame.'

'That's the way life pans out for all of us Barney,' she said. 'I never in my wildest dreams ever thought that my husband would end up this way and my son caught up in dealing drugs.'

Again Barney spoke softly to her well out of earshot from the back office. 'Anna look here, Glen was fitted up. When I see how Brian Wharton has prospered both in money terms and now in his marriage to Marlene there is only one conclusion I have come to. He needed to frame Glen to get himself out of big trouble with the organisation and then move in on his girlfriend. It was just pure envy on his part and from what I hear he treats that little girl like dirt.'

When Brian married Marlene both Derek and herself had not attended the wedding and her name was never mentioned when she was in conversation with her sister who was in effect Marlene's mother-in-law. Marlene had fell hook line and sinker believing the rumours surrounding Glen's involvement in the situation at The Liberty Arms on that fateful day three years before. Anna still harboured a grudge that Marlene's loyalty to her son was only paper thin and hence she avoided her in case she said something that she would regret.

Before the pair could continue their conversation the door of the rear office opened and Greg Bennet entered the bar. He had a look of surprise on his craggy face when he viewed Anna McElroy sitting on a chair opposite his barman. Barney rose up and went behind the bar counter to continue his preparations for the business of the day.

Bennet had an inkling why Anna had arrived at the bar this day but he asked in any case knowing full well she was there to plead to his better nature.

'And why do we have the pleasure of the company of Mrs. Anna McElroy this fine day?' he said with a smirk on his countenance.

'Take it from me it is no pleasure to be in your company,' barked Anna. 'It's only for the sake of my husband and son that I'm here at all.'

'Come into the office and we'll see what we can do for you,' replied Bennet attempting a conciliatory attitude.

Anna looked over at Barney who held both hands out with his palms in a downward position waving them up and down to signal her to stay cool once she would enter the office. Bennet sat down behind the desk and motioned the lady to sit down opposite him on a wooden chair. She looked around at the surroundings in the office and wondered why these men worked there in such spartan conditions when money was flowing in from their business of the supply of narcotics. Perhaps, she thought, it was to take any heat off them should the law decide to raid the premises. However, that hadn't happened as yet so the place was kept clean of drugs.

Greg Bennet broke the brief silence staring straight into Anna's face. 'Well what can I do for you?' he asked.

'As you probably know my husband is seriously ill and he has only three weeks at the most before this cancer takes him,' she said and with the words almost sticking in her throat she added, 'he wants to see his son one last time before he goes to meet his maker and I am asking you to lift this exclusion and allow Glen to come home to be with him.'

'Look Anna under the circumstances I'm prepared to be reasonable,' he replied with a faint smile on his face. 'If the upper echelons of the organisation are agreeable to this there will have to be certain conditions when he does come back.'

'And what would these so called conditions be?' she asked as her voice started to take on an angry tone.

'Firstly he will report to me here when he gets off the train and takes a taxi to the bar.' Bennet was in his element being able to lay down the law to the wife of Derek McElroy. 'Secondly, he stays well clear of his cousin Brian Wharton. I don't want any trouble out in the streets or in here and finally he has around two weeks only and reports back here when everything is finished.'

'When everything is finished as you so nicely put it I'm sure he will report back to complete his business with you before he goes back to Glasgow,' replied Anna.

Bennet looked at Anna quizzically. He was unsure if the last sentence emanating from her mouth was a veiled threat but he decided to let it go at that, just desiring the increasingly angry woman to get out of his presence.

'Tell him to see me next week when he arrives back from Glasgow,' he demanded and waved her away to leave the office.

Anna slammed the door and shook Barney's hand before leaving The Liberty Arms hoping she would never have to enter this run down place again. Instead of hailing a taxi she again decided to walk up the New Town Road thinking over what she was going to convey to her son over the phone. The wording of this conversation would have to be spelt out carefully as Glen would be most resentful in having to report to Bennet before he was able to see his parents and especially having to break his journey before going to the bedside of his gravely ill father. Anna hoped Glen would stay cool when he eventually arrived back in Drumfast.

CHAPTER FIVE
****

As the train slowly pulled into Drumfast Central Station Glen lifted his travel case off the seat beside him and prepared to step on to the platform once the train came to a stop. Walking along the concourse he marvelled at how the station had changed since he had left the same place three years before. The station had been given a complete makeover in the intervening period and it was unrecognisable from the dump it had been in the years before.

Glen hailed a taxi from the line of cabs awaiting the passengers exiting the train from Glasgow and hopped in beside the driver.

'Where to?' asked the middle aged driver who seemed glad to have some work to break the monotony from sitting listening to the banal chatter of an afternoon disc jockey.

'New Town Road mate,' Glen replied without adding the exact location on the two and a half mile thoroughfare.

'Tell me where on the road you want dropped off when we reach there,' added the cabbie.

'No problem,' said Glen and the journey proceeded in silence.

As the vehicle travelled over a bridge across the Drumfast River Glen noticed that the area where scrap metal had been piled up three years previously was now adorned with glass fronted office blocks. With the upgraded railway station and these new buildings it looked like the centre of the old town was being hauled into the twentieth century.

When the taxi pulled into the bottom end of the New Town Road Glen asked the driver to pull over to the side of the road and indicated that he would walk the short distance towards The Liberty Arms. He paid the cabbie the full fare plus the usual tip and exited the vehicle slinging his bag over his broad right shoulder.

Although he was anxious to get to his parent's residence there was no hurry reporting to Bennet and he wanted to see what the road looked like since he had left the city those three years before. Although the railway station and the riverside area had been improved the same could not be said of the New Town Road. It seemed that every other shop was boarded up which was testament to a cost of living crisis and the exodus of people moving out to the new housing estates on the suburbs of the city much like his own parents had done. It was obvious that decent people were glad to see the back of the rampant drug dealing that Bennet and his cohorts were still peddling in the district.

As he started walking along the road the words of a song much favoured by his father came into his mind. It was called 'Bad Boy' by a singer called Marty Wilde and he felt that the words of the first line of verse one suited himself down to the ground. *'Well the people down the street whoever you meet say I'm a bad boy.'* A lot of people up and down the streets of the district had indeed tarnished him with the brush of a drug dealer although some of the more informed citizens always had grave doubts on that score.

The song kept swirling through his head as he jauntily strode along the road gazing right and left at the windows of the shops that were still open and then glancing down the streets of terraced houses on the opposite side of the road. In no time at all he was at the door of The Liberty Arms and he straightened himself up to his full height before entering the bar.

Glen entered the bar and immediately turned his head to the left and looked for the table where he was last seated on that fateful evening before his exile. A red mist descended over his mind when he viewed his cousin Brian Wharton sitting there playing cards with his friend Jordy. Wharton dropped his head when he saw who was glaring over at him. From past experience he knew he had come off second best when the pair had settled any differences with their fists in any convenient alleyway. He was hoping to avoid a similar altercation on this day.

It was only the voice of Barney the barman that stopped him from rushing over and upending the table with his cousin and possibly his friend ending up underneath it.

'Glen son, don't do it,' said the older man in a soothing voice. 'He's not worth it. You'll only undo the good work your mother has done in getting you here to be by your father's side.'

Barney's intervention seemed to do the trick as Glen flashed one last glare over at the table in the corner and turned his back on the pair at the table to talk to the friendly barman.

'My goodness Glen,' said the relieved Barney, 'you certainly have put on the muscle since you have been living in Glasgow. Where has that skinny seventeen year old gone to.'

'I've been going to the gym to work out twice a week,' informed Glen. 'Glasgow can be a tough city at times so I have learned the hard way to look after myself especially on Rangers/Celtic match days. The hatred of the supporters of old firm hasn't subsided even after all these years.'

'Of that I'm sure lad. I could see the fear in your cousin's face when you walked in the door,' laughed the barman as he dried a glass with a clean dish cloth. 'Why that girl Marlene married him I cannot understand because he spends most of his waking hours in this bar drinking, dealing and chatting up women if they'll give him the time of day.'

'Well that was her choice,' replied Glen. 'Like most of the crowd around here she believed every rumour that was spread around the district. I believe her mother pushed her into the marriage. Is that true?'

'So I heard,' said Barney. 'Brian Wharton went on a charm offensive in the beginning of the relationship but once he got her hooked it was back to his normal self.'

'So, that's her funeral. I'm well over it now,' added Glen.

Barney smiled at that remark for he knew that Marlene had regretted her decision to marry Brian after a couple of months when he reverted to his previous lifestyle of being a single man to all intents and purposes. The barman could see Wharton's behaviour each and every night when he was at his usual table drinking and carousing in The Liberty Arms. It was obvious that the main thrust of winning Marlene was to get one over on his cousin Glen. To Brian this was a major victory to supersede all the knock backs he had taken from his present wife in the past.

Glen's voice interrupted Barney's thoughts of the past. 'I suppose I'll have to go to the hovel that he calls an office and see what that twat Bennet has to say,' he said.

Before he made a move to walk to the back office Eddie McGaughey appeared and walked over to the bar counter. He pointed to the optics on the wall without saying a word to the barman and Barney filled two tumblers with whiskey.

Glen looked him up and down. He hadn't changed much from that last time they had encountered each other. The slight limp was still there but his almost square shaped body still emitted menace as he moved over to the bar counter. McGaughey, however, noticed the much more filled out and muscled appearance of the young man standing before him. Someone who may not be pushed around this time like the thin teenager who left the city three years before.

'You had better get into the office pronto,' said McGaughey. 'Greg doesn't like to be kept waiting especially by the likes of you.'

'Well he's been waiting three long years for this moment so another couple of minutes won't hurt him,' replied Glen raising himself up once again to his full height from leaning against the bar counter.

'Just get in there and none of your smart talk or it'll be the worse for you,' threatened McGaughey.

A smile broke out on Glen's face as he purposely brushed against McGaughey's shoulder spilling half of the drink from one of the tumblers. Bennet's sidekick was almost incandescent with rage and he ordered Barney to fill the glass up once again.

'Sorry about that Eddie,' said the grinning Glen. 'How much was that whiskey Barney, I'll pay for that spillage.'

'You needn't bother,' shouted the angry McGaughey, 'just get into the office to see Greg and get your orders for the next few weeks.'

'Yes sir,' said Glen sarcastically as if he was a servant attending to his master, 'Can I carry your whiskey glasses in for you sir.'

'You mind your tongue or you'll be on the next train to Glasgow or wherever you've been living,' said McGaughey.

'I'll leave that decision to the organ grinder not the monkey,' replied Glen as he once again brushed past McGaughey almost spilling the drink once again.

He didn't wait for Eddie McGaughey to proceed in front of him but pushed the office door open to view Bennet sitting at the same old desk as he had been behind the three years before. Greg Bennet had lost weight since their last encounter. This time he was clean shaven which highlighted the high colouring of his face with his nose having a mottled appearance due to years of heavy drinking.

Bennet looked up from reading a document and a look of surprise came into his face when he viewed the much more mature and manly Glen McElroy standing before the desk. He knew Glen's reputation as someone in the past who could more than hold his own if he was attacked by some other youth. By the look of him now he would be a formidable opponent in a one to one scrap with anyone just like his father Derek in his prime.

Bennet went on a charm offensive attempting to bring a civilised atmosphere into the proceedings.

'Sorry to hear about your father,' he said. 'That is why I have attempted to persuade the bosses of the organisation to allow you come back to be with him. But there will be conditions.'

'And what would those be?' asked Glen.

'You stay well away from your cousin and his wife and once the funeral of your father is over you leave Drumfast once again, this time for good.' It looked like Bennet was not intending to allow any further latitude for the loss of Glen's father.

'Make sure you heed what Greg is saying,' added Eddie McGaughey and looking at Bennet he added, 'this young numpty tried to be smart with me in front of Barney at the bar counter. He was lucky I didn't deck him there and then.'

Glen laughed and Bennet was aware that the chance of a fracas in the office was a distinct possibility so he was determined to nip it in the bud right away.

'Just shut up Eddie,' he commanded and looking over at Glen he added 'It is out of respect for your father that you are allowed to come back here. Just keep your nose clean over the next couple of weeks. Now get out and come back here once the business is finished at your house. I'll have a taxi waiting to take you to the station and back to Glasgow.'

'Very considerate of you,' said Glen sarcastically as he turned on his heel slamming the office door hard when he left and entered the bar. He flashed a mean glare over at Brian Wharton who once again dropped his head and continued the pretence of dealing cards to his companion.

'Good to see you again Barney,' he said as he passed the bar counter.

'And you too son,' replied the old barman. 'Look after yourself and give my regards to your dad. If I get a chance I'll come up to see him.'

'That would be good,' replied Glen. 'You'll be most welcome.'

It looked like Bennet's charm offensive did not have any soothing effect on Glen and the thought of revenge was starting to well up in his mind. However, that would have to wait as he was anxious to reach his parent's house to be with his father and support his mother. He walked up the New Town Road and entered the taxi cab office to wait for the next available vehicle to take him home to the residence where he was born.

CHAPTER SIX
****

The taxi drew up outside the semi-detached dwelling that had been Glen's home before he was forced into exile in Glasgow three years before. As he opened the wrought iron gate and walked up the short path a sense of sadness enveloped him as he thought back to the past at how hard his parents had worked to buy the house. His father had only enjoyed living there intermittently as due to the lack of contracts in his home area he was forced to regularly work abroad to put food on the table and pay the mortgage as well as dealing with the utility bills.

Since his illness had struck him down Derek and Anna had been living off their savings and the mere pittance that the state provided. It was fortunate that Glen had been earning good money in Glasgow so he was able to send something back to supplement his parents living expenses due to their reduced circumstances.

As he looked up at the red brick building he could see a bright light reflecting through the venetian blinds in the front bedroom which had always been his parent's sleeping quarters. He guessed that in this very room his father would be receiving palliative care for the remaining weeks of his life.

He opened the front door which was unlocked and walked up the hall to where he could see a light coming from the kitchen. When he looked in to his annoyance standing there stirring soup was his Aunt Sarah. There was no welcome back from Brian Wharton's mother as both stared hard at each other waiting for the other to speak. There was no smile on her stern face and when Sarah eventually broke the silence there was nothing conciliatory in her voice.

'I don't want you coming back here and stirring up trouble for your parents and especially with my Brian,' she said. 'He has been living a good life and is in a very happy marriage so you should stay well away from him and Marlene.'

'Look Sarah, I've not come back here to be lectured by you,' retorted Glen. 'Maybe you have been a great help my mum so I will say nothing about Brian or Marlene in the meantime but mark my words I have a lot of things to clear up before I go back to Glasgow. If I do go back.'

'Is that a threat?' asked Sarah.

'No, it is a promise,' replied Glen as he left the kitchen and headed slowly up the stairs to see his father. This was a moment he had been dreading as he was unaware what condition his dad would be in due to the ravages of his illness.

He opened the bedroom door where his mother was sitting on the edge of the bed talking to her beloved Derek. When she saw Glen standing there she jumped up and threw her arms around him in a warm embrace. As he looked over his mother's shoulder he was shocked to see his father sitting up in the bed smiling at him but was now looking more like a genial skeleton as his weight had plummeted over the preceding months. His striped pyjamas seemed to hang on his now emaciated body.

The room looked completely different from the last time he had been in there. As well as a hospital type bed in the middle of the front wall of the room a commode chair sat on one side of the bed denoting that his father was now too weak to make it to the toilet along the landing. On the dressing table sat an array of various tablets which were there to ensure that the patient could spend his last days without having to bear the excruciating pain in his stomach.

Anna and Glen broke away from their embrace and he went over to the bed. As he gently placed his arms around his dad all he could feel was the rib cage of his father's body. The pent up emotions over the past few hours flooded out from him as the tears rolled down his face. His father put his hands on both Glen's shoulders and summoning all his strength to hold him at arm's length.

'Listen here son, I don't want any blubbing and weeping,' he said. 'You need to be strong and brave to get your mother through this. I've already told her the same.'

'I'll try my best dad. Is there anything I can do for you when I am here?' asked Glen.

'I will leave you two to have a yarn and go down to see if Sarah has finished making the soup.' said Anna as she blew a kiss at the two men from the bedroom door.

Derek waited until his wife had got out of earshot and with a bit of effort pulled a sheet of A4 paper from below one of the pillows at the head of the bed. His hand was shaking as he scanned the paper and he then sat it in front of him on the bed.

'There are three things I want you to do for me,' he said. 'The first one is to pass yourself off with your Aunt Sarah. I know you and her have never had much time for each other but she has been a great help to your mother so just stay cool no matter what she says.'

'I'll try my best dad but she has already fired a salvo across my bows as soon as I entered the house,' Glen pleaded.

'I'm sure you fired one back at her. Anyway do your best to keep things peaceful. The second and a very important thing is arranging my funeral,' said Derek.

The words 'arranging my funeral' struck Glen like a dagger thrusting through his heart. He had never, in his wildest dreams, thought he would be put in this position but he was his father's only son and he would be looked upon to undertake this mission. His father could sense that Glen was taken aback by his request and moved to assure the young man that he would not be on his own in this regard.

'Look Glen your Uncle Andy is arriving here next week or maybe before if I don't make it that far so he will help and advise you to make all the necessary arrangements.' said Derek trying to reassure his son that help would be on the way. And maybe your cousin Brian could help in some small way under the circumstances.'

'The only way he can help is staying well out of my way,' said Glen. 'Uncle Andy and I will do just fine. So what is the third thing you want me to do dad?'

Derek handed the sheet of paper he had recovered from below the pillow over to Glen and his son proceeded to read the contents which looked as if they had been written some time before illness had struck his father down. The sheet contained the lyrics of a song Derek had composed when he whiled away the time when working in the middle east a few years before. His father was as hard as nails in his prime but Glen was impressed as he scanned down the verses and the sentiments they expressed. The words of the lyrics rang true to what was happening in Drumfast due to the mushrooming drug problem and how it was affecting the young people and the older citizens of that city.

Once again as he read over the lyrics it struck him that they could also apply to him personally. Maybe not. His father was probably thinking about the situation in his home city when he wrote the song.

It was entitled 'This Land Is Not a Home' and he read it out loud to his father to comfort him in the knowledge that he was impressed with this latent talent.

> 'This land is not a home
> Til everyone is free
> To live their lives the way
> They want it to be
> To make the choice
> Between what's right and wrong
> And to give them
> The feeling that they belong
>
> > Let's make them welcome
> > Make then glad
> > That they are
> > Safe with us forever
> > And in time I'm sure
> > They'll help us if they can.
>
> Why can't we show
> Some love and charity
> In their welfare
> Our interest make them believe
> And in the end
> I'm sure that we will find
> We will all be blessed
> With happier minds
>
> > Chorus: Let's make them welcome etc
>
> So easy to think
> This plea is surely lost
> In a cold cold world
> Where life has little cost
> But if two foes shake hands
> And end the fight
> Maybe some day soon
> Their friends may see the light

LAST SONG FOR A RETURNING EXILE

Chorus: Let's make them welcome etc

This land is not a home
Til everyone is free
To live their lives the way
They want it to be
To make the choice
Between what's right and wrong
And to give them
The feeling that they belong

Chorus: Let's make them welcome etc'

Glen looked over at his father who seemed a trifle embarrassed as he listened to the words he had composed being read out aloud. He moved to reassure the dying man that he was impressed with this talent that had been hidden for so long.

'Dad I knew you were a keen music fan but you kept this writing lark a bit quiet. You said there was a third thing you wanted me to do. Is it something regarding this song?' he asked.

'Yes. I think you know an old pal of mine called Fred Jenkinson,' said Derek attempting to raise himself upright on the bed.

'He has a radio show on Radio Drumfast,' replied Glen. 'Uncle Andy listens to him on his FM radio in Glasgow. I think he goes by the name of Jinky Jenkinson when he is on the air.'

'That's right. The name Jinky sounds a lot more showbiz than plain Fred. Anyway he has announced on his radio show that there is going to be a song contest next week in the Drumfast Central Hall and the organisers are looking for original songs from people in the district.' Derek was gasping and had to pause to get a breath so Glen waited until he had composed himself once again.

'Just take it easy dad,' he said in a comforting voice. 'Try not to take too much out of yourself.'

Derek waited for a moment and proceeded to issue further instructions to his son. 'Fred or Jinky, as you know him by, finishes his show around midday on week days. If you wait outside the radio station give that paper to him and introduce yourself. He will barely recognise you now as the last time the two of you met you were only a slip of a boy.'

'How can he help to submit this song?' asked Glen. 'I mean there is just words and no music for it.'

'That's where Fred comes in,' gasped Derek. 'He was the lead guitarist in a pop group before getting the job of presenting a show on the radio. He is able to read and indeed write music. When he knows who this is for I'm confident he will gladly help out. We went to school together and when we left and started work both of us went to dances together and that was where I met your mother.'

'Did you lose track of each other then?' asked Glen.

'You know how it is,' added Derek. 'I married your mother and concentrated on making a living and Jinky went full time with the band and toured all over the place which meant we went our separate ways.'

Glen could see that his father was getting tired and had probably done more talking in the past half hour than he had uttered all day.

'Could you help me to get down a bit more flatter on the bed son?' Derek asked as his son moved closer.

When he placed his arms around his father's emaciated body it once again distressed him when he could feel the bones of Derek's ribcage against his arms as he laid his father down on the bed. After he had helped Derek into a more relaxed position he folded the paper, kissed his father on the forehead and left the room determined to carry out the dying man's wishes.

He was mightily relieved when he entered the kitchen to find Aunt Sarah had left for home. The less he saw of her the better. If she started to extol the virtues of her son Brian he was liable to blow a fuse and he desired to avoid a toxic atmosphere which could prevail in those circumstances especially with a gravely ill man in the upstairs bedroom. It wasn't beyond the bounds of possibility that she would attempt to provoke him to prove that, in her mind, he hadn't changed since his period in exile.

A hot bowl of vegetable soup and a fresh cheese sandwich soon put the thoughts of his vindictive aunt out of his mind as he settled down to enjoy the company of his mother and plan the next move regarding bringing his father's song to fruition. Anna knew Fred Jenkinson from years past so she wrote a letter of introduction in case he thought Glen was some sort of crank accosting him outside the radio station.

As he looked over at her composing the note Glen noticed how tired and haggard looking she had become with the strain of nursing his father over the past months. Even though a district nurse paid visits every day to dispense medication, for the majority of the time it was left to Anna to fetch and willingly carry out the task of comforting her husband in the final period of his life.

'If Jinky doesn't recognise you, give him this note,' she said. 'Even though your dad and him hadn't seen each other very regularly over the past number of years I'm sure he will help to undertake this final wish for his old friend.'

'I certainly hope so Mum,' replied Glen. 'Dad seems think that this will be the last item in his bucket list.'

Anna sadly nodded her head. It was breaking his heart to be losing his father but what must it be like for her to have to part with her life's partner, love and best friend. The thought of her being on her own once his father passed away was also tearing him apart inside.

The day passed by with Glen unpacking his suitcase and once again feeling at home in his childhood bedroom. He sat chatting with his mother for the rest of the afternoon and in the evening helped her to make Derek a light meal and then watch television until the late evening news ended.

'I'm going up to give your dad his final meds for the night,' said Anna. 'Then I'm off to bed,'

'I'll not be too long after you. Goodnight Mum sleep well,' said Glen as he kissed his mother on the forehead and watched her walk in a tired fashion towards the stairs. The resolve was emerging in his mind that somehow this exile must come to an end. It was either Greg Bennet and himself who must come out on top once the two week's grace would come to an end and he would be expected to leave once again for Glasgow. Glen was determined that it would be him who would somehow prevail before that period would end and he would once again be back living in Drumfast for good.

CHAPTER SEVEN
****

The bus drove into the city centre square and stopped at the row of bus stops along the edge of the pavement. Glen waited his turn to get off as the queue of passengers in front of him alighted to go about their business in the shops and offices of the Drumfast commercial area.

He crossed the busy road at the traffic lights and walked down the street that led to the premises of Radio Drumfast FM. When the hundred yards was completed he entered the station and sat down on one of the many seats provided for people who, on occasions, made up the audience for live recordings of talk shows which made up the evening programming at the station. He listened as two speakers blared out the finish of a tune and as it faded the voice of the man he had come to see announced the end of his show.

'That's your lot for today folks,' the voice said. 'This is Jinky Jenkinson wishing you all a great afternoon and I will see you at the same time bright and early at nine o'clock tomorrow morning. Right now here is the twelve o'clock news from Radio Drumfast FM.'

Glen waited for around ten minutes half listening to the news which was highlighting the growing drug problem in the city. It was reporting that the law enforcement agencies were fighting an ongoing battle with the drugs gangs but it seemed that stalemate had prevailed. Lack of evidence seemed to ensure that the likes of Greg Bennet and Eddie McGaughey could evade the clutches of the law with impunity by overlording a system of fear in the New Town Road district of Drumfast.

His slight attention to the news was broken by the sound of the elevator arriving on the ground floor. When it opened a tall thick set man wearing a black baseball cap appeared. He was dressed in a leather jacket with a lime coloured shirt tucked into his pale blue jeans. His perma-tanned face, complete with a pencil thin moustache, creased into a smile as he gave a cheery wave to the girl at the reception desk. To all intents and purposes it looked like he was trying to push Old Father Time as far back as was possible given he was fifty-four years of age.

'Good show today Jinky,' she complimented him which made an even broader grin cover his countenance.

'Thanks a lot Judith,' he replied. 'Leave me a note for a request tomorrow morning and I will slip it into the show for you.'

'I will indeed,' she said and continued to type at her computer.

Glen rose up and approached the man holding the paper containing the song lyrics and the introductory note from his mother. Jinky was under the impression that this was an autograph hunter craving his signature. He would be only too glad to oblige as these fans were few and far between since the heady days when he had recorded and played gigs with the Drumfast Casuals around the dance halls and clubs in the city and its surrounds.

As Glen approached him Jinky pulled out a pen from his inside jacket pocket and presumed the young man desired an autograph.

'What message would you like me to put on one of the pieces of the paper you have there son?' he asked.

'Sadly I'm not here to get an autograph,' replied Glen. 'Maybe this note will explain everything.'

Jinky was getting curious and took the paper from the outstretched hand of Glen and started to read the message from Anna, Glen's mother. Suddenly a smile broke into his face.

'So you are Derek McElroy's boy,' he said eventually looking up from the note. 'The last time I saw you young man you could hardly reach up to my knee cap when I bumped into your dad holding your hand on the New Town Road.'

'A lot of things have changed especially for myself and my father since those days,' said Glen sadly as he shook Jinky's hand.

'Let's go and take a seat in the corner over there and you can let me know all about Derek, your Mum and the reason for your visit here today,' the radio presenter said warmly.

When they sat down Glen explained the situation regarding his exile in Glasgow but more importantly the state of his father's failing health. Noting the sudden downcast expression on Jinky's face he handed over the sheet of paper containing the words of the song Derek had written. The older man quickly scanned down the page at first then once again read over the words written on it.

'What do you want me to do with this?' he asked as he laid it down on his lap and waited for an answer from Glen.

'It looks like my dad is good with words but he can't write music and he needs a melody, or whatever you call it. A tune to go with the verses,' explained Glen. 'One of his last wishes is for this song to be entered into a contest which I believe will take place in a week or so.'

'That's right,' said Jinky. 'But really I can't enter the contest because the station is one of the sponsors and it is being broadcast there.'

'So he is sunk then,' added Glen dejectedly and as he got up to leave Jenkinson pulled him down into the chair again.

Jinky thought for a moment and then came up with a suggestion. 'I could compose a tune but it would need to be on the quiet whereby my name is kept right out of it. Your dad will have to take all the credit,' he added with a smile on his tanned face.

'Look, that would be fantastic,' said Glen. 'Would it take you long to make up a tune?'

'I have a couple of jingles to record this afternoon for my show,' the presenter said, 'but after that I'm off home. Seeing it's Derek I'll work on it right away as the deadline for entrants is in three day's time. I take it that this is the home address on your mother's note.'

'Fantastic! Yes it is. Look, thanks a lot for this.' exclaimed Glen as he rose up and shook the hand of the man who was in the pole position to deliver one of the last wishes of his dying father.

Glen almost skipped out of the radio station with delight and hoped that he would not have to wait too long for a bus to transport him back home with the good news that Derek's friend from the past was going to make his dream become a reality. It was with mixed emotions that he sat and gazed out the window of the bus wishing his father's ambition to have a song performed, or even recorded, had been realised much earlier in Derek's life. At least now his father could pass away in the knowledge that this final item on his bucket list had been fulfilled and could be ticked off.

As the bus passed along the New Town Road it pulled into a stop just adjacent to The Liberty Arms to pick up some passengers. Glen looked out the window and viewed his cousin Brian and his mate Jordy Andrews having a smoke outside the premises. He stared directly out at the pair and wondered what they were inhaling, probably something other than tobacco. Just as the bus was about to continue its journey Brian looked up and spied Glen staring out of the window at him and his friend. Brian nudged Jordy and fearing that his cousin might hop off the bus to finally take revenge on him for his past act of treachery the pair quickly entered the sanctuary of the public house just in case.

Any revenge would have to wait until another day. In the meantime it was satisfying enough that Brian Wharton was having to keep looking over his shoulder wondering when the hammer of justice was going to strike down on his head from his cousin. When the bus stopped close to the street where the family lived Glen was anxious to get home and spread the good news of his meeting with Jinky Jenkinson. He sprinted along the pavement, opened the gate and entered through the front door. Just as he was about to ascend the stairs his mother appeared from the kitchen with a worried look on her pale face.

'Glen, the nurse is with your father at the moment,' she said. 'He had a bad night with the pain and she thinks they may have to increase the medication to control it. Just hold on until she comes down and then you can go up. How did you get on with Fred Jenkinson?'

'Good,' he replied. 'He is going to write some music to the words but it will have to be kept secret about his involvement. He would be compromised if it was discovered that he had anything to do with the song. There's a chance he could lose his job if it came out that he was involved in this as the radio station is one of the main sponsors of the contest.'

'That is so kind of him,' replied Anna. 'Fred and your Dad go back a long way from their school days. He was with your father when we met at a dance but soon afterwards he joined the group and started touring everywhere. It meant that we lost contact with him over the years.'

'Well it looks like that contact is going to be resumed Mum,' said Glen. 'Jinky is going to work on the tune right away and he has our address so he could be here within the next couple of days.'

'I certainly hope so,' replied Anna, 'because time is slipping away so fast and so is your father.'

Anna started sobbing and Glen held her in his arms to give her some sort of comfort. She composed herself when she heard the nurse descending the stairs and waited to hear what condition her husband was in at that moment.

'He's a bit more comfortable now Mrs. McElroy,' informed the nurse. 'I'll be back tomorrow morning and we'll see if the additional meds are doing the trick in the meantime.'

'Thanks nurse that is good to know,' said Anna.

Derek was now comfortable and the slight additional dose of morphine gave the opportunity to enable him to live with the pain until the nurse would return the next morning. Anna accompanied the lady to the front door and watched as she drove away down the street in her Morris Minor probably to administer medication to another gravely ill patient. She turned and looked at her son standing at the foot of the stairs almost waiting for permission to go up to see his father.

'Right, let's go up and give him the good news about the song,' she declared as she led the way up to the bedroom.

'Well how did it go with Fred?' asked Derek attempting to raise himself up to hear the news of the meeting.

'It went very well Dad,' replied Glen. 'He is going to work on a tune right away.'

'That's good,' gasped Derek who once again slumped back on the bed after Anna and Glen placed the pillows at his back to get him into a more comfortable position. 'I'm looking forward to seeing Fred again and hear what he has done to the song.'

'So are we Derek,' said Anna. 'Now try to get some sleep and conserve your energy.'

'I will,' smiled Derek as he closed his eyes in the contented knowledge that his last ambition had a more than even chance of being realised.

CHAPTER EIGHT
****

It was late evening two days later when a knock came to the door and Glen rushed down the hall to open the door thinking it may have been Jinky Jenkinson arriving with the completed song ready to be entered in the contest. To his extreme disappointment it was his Aunt Sarah so he stood back and let her pass by him in the hall without both saying a word of welcome or otherwise.

Sarah peeped into the kitchen and when she saw that her sister was not there she mounted the stairs to find out the condition of her brother-in-law knowing Anna would probably be sitting there with him. Glen waited in the living room not wishing whatsoever to be in the company of an aunt who over the years had never a good word to say about him even before the situation with the drugs in The Liberty Arms had reared its ugly head.

It was just rank jealousy on Sarah's part that he had forged a career in the printing industry while her son Brian's only ambition was to live off the state by claiming unemployment benefit whilst unknown to her he was supplementing his income by dealing narcotics for the organisation. This was something her son had been able to conceal from her over the years even though she must have wondered how he was able to finance a lifestyle far above what he received on the dole.

After around a half an hour he heard his mother and aunt coming down the stairs and he was anxious she would leave before Jinky might arrive with the finished song. The fewer people who knew about the radio presenter's involvement the better it would be for all concerned. It was with immense relief when he heard the front door being opened and his mother bidding her sister farewell.

'What did she want?' asked Glen as his mother popped her head around the living room door.

'She just wanted to find out how your dad is doing,' replied Anna. 'Glen, I just wish you would pass yourself with her. She has been a great help to me over the past couple of months.'

'Respect works both ways Mum,' he said forcefully. 'I mean she never had any time for me even when I was a kid and just earlier tonight she swanned past me without saying a word.'

Anna decided to leave the topic by just adding, 'it is so sad that things have to be like this especially at this time.'

Before Glen could answer another knock resounded from the front door and this time Anna rushed to answer in case her sister had forgotten something and she was anxious to avoid another stand off between Sarah and her son.

However, when she opened the door standing there was a blast from the past, none other than Fred Jenkinson or Jinky as he was better known in present times. A smile light up his tanned face as he viewed the woman motioning him to enter the house.

'Anna McElroy, still as pretty as ever,' he enthused ignoring the fact that her appearance had changed somewhat since the last time he was in her company and not for the better.

'Fred so good to see you again,' she said. 'Derek will be happy that you have decided to help him in this last ambition.'

'No problem,' Fred replied, 'and where is that big strapping son of yours?'

When Glen heard Jinky's voice he appeared from the living room and shook the visitor's hand very warmly.

'I've brought a CD with me,' the presenter said. 'I take it you have a player somewhere?'

'Yes there is one beside Derek's bed,' replied Anna. 'When he has one of his better days he likes to listen to one of his favourite albums.'

'Good,' said Jinky with a broad smile on his face. 'Young man you lead the way and we'll see if your dad is happy with what I have done to his words.'

When the three climbed the stairs and entered the bedroom the smile quickly left Jenkinson's face when he viewed his old mate lying on the bed. The big strapping man that was Derek McElroy was a gaunt human being whose pyjamas appeared to be two sizes too big for him due to the ravages of his illness.

In contrast a smile encompassed Derek's countenance when he saw the old friend from his school and teenage days standing at the end of the bed. He tried to raise himself up to a sitting position but was unable to summon up enough strength to do so. Glen and Anna rushed over and were able to assist him to sit upright placing four pillows at his back to support him in that position.

'Fred I'm so glad to see you again,' gasped Derek and in a reference to Sarah, his previous visitor, he added. 'This has made my day having someone that I really like come to visit me.'

'You may not be so glad when you hear what I have done to your song. I have it here on a compact disc,' joked Fred as he took a seat aside the bed.

'Look Fred you were always a talented guy, I'm sure it will be fine. Glen switch the CD player on.' replied Derek, summoning up as much enthusiasm as he could muster under the circumstances.

Glen slid the compact disc into the player and the company waited with bated breath for the sound to come out of the internal speaker of the machine. The piano and guitar intro lasted twelve seconds before the voice of Fred Jenkinson filled the room singing the words that Derek had composed.

Anna noticed that her husband had tears in his eyes and she moved over and placed her arm around his shoulder feeling a mixture sadness and pride at the same time. Glen listened in wonderment until the final notes of the song drifted out from the player and the four people in the room sat in quiet contemplation until Derek broke the silence.

'Fred, my old mate, you have done me proud,' he said wiping the tears from his eyes with a paper tissue that Anna had given him.

'The old voice is not what it used to be. Too many years of inhaling nicotine and bawling out rock songs..' Jinky replied, 'but there again I won't be singing it in the competition.'

'Who will be performing it?' asked Glen. 'Do we present the CD to the organisers?'

'No way!' said Fred. 'They would twig on right away it was my bawling voice on the disc. I have written the notes and words on a manuscript and there will be a choir and a five-piece band performing the competing songs on the night of the contest.'

He placed his hand into his inside overcoat pocket and pulled out a folded brown envelope which he handed to Glen. The young man opened the flap and pulled out the white A4 sheet and looked in amazement at the format of music notes and words filling most of the area on the paper. His admiration for his father's old friend knew no bounds as he placed it once again into the envelope.

Fred Jenkinson rose up from his seat and prepared to leave. He looked sadly at his buddy from past glory days lying helplessly on the hospital type bed and somehow regretted that their paths had not crossed more regularly in recent years and in a better situation.

'Make sure you take that envelope down to the Central Hall by twelve o'clock tomorrow,' he said addressing his comment to Glen. 'That is the deadline and like anyone presenting a tender for work they won't accept it a minute after that time.'

'Don't worry Fred,' added Anna. 'I'll have Glen up bright and early and he will be on the first bus into the city centre.'

'Good!' replied Fred and once again looking over at Derek he said. 'If I get the chance I'll come to listen to the contest next week on the radio with you mate.'

'That's if I'm still here,' replied Derek attempting to add some levity into the proceedings.

'You had better be here or I have wasted my time with this song,' quipped Fred and with a wave of his hand he left the room trying hard to fight back the tears from streaming down his cheeks.

Glen accompanied him downstairs and escorted his father's old friend to the front door.

'I can't thank you enough for this,' said Glen holding out the brown envelope.

'Just make sure you get it there in good time,' replied Jinky Jenkinson and with a cheery wave of his hand he strolled down the path and hopped into his car.

Glen watched as the vehicle turned the corner of the street. He closed the front door and ascended the stairs once again wishing to say goodnight to his parents. An early night was in order as he needed to be on the first bus to the city centre the next morning and lodge his father's entrant into the Drumfast Song Contest by the midday deadline.

He popped his head into the bedroom and bade his mother and father a fond goodnight before getting himself ready to be fresh and bushy-tailed by having a good night's sleep for the expedition the next morning.

CHAPTER NINE
****

Glen woke the following morning to the sound of his mother banging on his bedroom door. He rubbed the sleep from his eyes and lazily swung his legs over the edge of the single bed. There was a slight fear that his father had taken a bad turn in the night but it was with immense relief that his mother announced that breakfast was ready in the kitchen.

After a quick shower he pulled on a pale yellow shirt and donned a pair of light blue jeans before hopping down the stairs and pulling on a pair of slip-on shoes which his mother had meticulously cleaned for his expedition into the Drumfast city centre. This was a huge part of the home comforts he sorely missed during his years of exile in Scotland namely his mother's undivided attention to his mode of dress and general welfare.

'How did Dad get on last night?' Glen asked as he tucked in to a bowl of Shredded Wheat.

'I went in a couple of times but he slept most of the night,' replied Anna. 'The nurse will be here in another half an hour to monitor his pain relief.'

'Look Mum I will start sitting by him at night to give you a break. You look done out,' he added.

'At the moment you just concentrate in getting that envelope into town in good time,' she asserted. 'Then we can work out a rota for night time. Anyway your Uncle Andy will be here at the weekend so it will take a bit of the strain off us. The only worry is how he and Sarah will get on.'

'Knowing Uncle Andy he will pass himself with her,' added Glen. 'After all she is his sister as well as you.'

'You don't know the half of it,' said Anna. 'As the eldest in the family she made his life a misery when we were all living at home. That is why he left for Glasgow. I'll tell you all about it some time in the future.'

'Strange he never ever spoke about it all the time I have been living with him. Although I often wondered why he left this city for Glasgow,' added Glen.

'Enough about my family's past history, you had better get ready and get moving to catch that bus.' There was no way Anna was going to elaborate or otherwise in her past family history at this juncture. The present was more important than family interactions in the distant past.

Anna had Glen's leather jacket hanging on the chair back and when he put it on he checked that the envelope containing the manuscript was intact in the inside pocket. Kissing his mother on the cheek he sprinted out the front door and made his way quickly up the street and ascended the slight incline leading to the bus stop. When the bus arrived he paid the fare and took his seat on the right side of the lower deck so that he could see if there was any movement at the bar where his troubles had started those three long years ago.

The bus trundled its way along the New Town Road moving much slower than he would have liked. As it inched by The Liberty Arms he watched as Barney raised the metal shutter to open up for another day of pulling pints and serving bar snacks to the punters who frequented the establishment.

He looked at his watch and it showed the time of a quarter past eleven which meant that the bus should arrive at the city centre bus stop in approximately ten minutes time. This would give him thirty-five minutes to lodge the song application in Drumfast Central Hall, plenty of time in normal travel conditions. But today there was an abnormal amount of traffic on the road leading to the city centre and the bus was only edging a few yards at a time in the long line of vehicles.

After a while Glen looked at his watch once again and the hands had moved again showing that the time was now twenty five minutes to twelve. At this rate it would be doubtful if the bus would reach the terminus in the city centre before midday as it crawled slowly along the thoroughfare. He made the snap decision to alight from the bus and make his way on foot to the venue in the city centre.

After moving to the front of the bus he spoke to the driver. 'Any chance you could let me off here mate?' he asked. 'I need to get to the city centre before twelve.'

'I really shouldn't let you off here but just watch the traffic coming up on the inside lane,' advised the driver as he opened the door to allow Glen to hop out. He looked to his left to make sure he was not wiped out by a passing car on the inside and jumped on to the pavement just before a line of cars drove up along the side of the bus.

As he ran along the pavement he came upon the reason for the traffic jam. An ambulance was in the centre of the road and two badly damaged cars sat at almost a right angles to each other. They had obviously collided when one of them had decided to change lanes at the last moment. The consternation of the walking wounded was obvious as they looked at the more seriously injured passengers being carried into the ambulance on stretchers by the paramedics.

Glen pushed his way through the crowd of rubbernecking people on the pavement and sprinted onwards towards his final destination. There was still a fair distance to travel and it would be nip and tuck if he were to reach the central hall in time to lodge the manuscript. Eventually he reached the city centre at ten minutes to twelve. There was a set of traffic lights to cross and there seemed to be an absolute eternity as the traffic streamed by and the green man on the traffic sign opposite was not appearing to allow him to cross. He decided there was no alternative but to take his chance and nip in between the moving cars and lorries as the time had moved on to seven minutes to twelve.

The vehicle horns blasted and vehicles braked as he weaved in and out of the slow moving traffic. It was fortunate that no custodians of the law were in the vicinity as he would have been arrested for jaywalking. The astonished onlookers watched with open mouths as he sprinted onwards towards the Drumfast Central Hall. With perspiration streaming down his face he entered the building with two minutes to spare.

A matronly looking woman was sitting at a table in the reception area. She looked up and down at the flushed young man from head to toe as if he was something that the cat had dragged in. Glen placed the envelope on the table in front of her.

'You have certainly cut this a bit fine,' she said without a hint of a smile. She opened the envelope and proceeded to examine the contents.

'You don't know the half of it,' Glen replied and gasped with relief when she intimated that everything was in order and placed the envelope into a tray containing other similar documents.

Before he left the hall Glen looked at a roll up banner stand advertising the song contest. It noted that all the songs were to be performed by the Drumfast Gospel Choir accompanied by a five-piece band just as Jinky had said. There was just one problem when he read on down to the smaller print near the bottom. Only the ten best selected songs would be entered into the contest final so there was a chance that his father's song would not be heard when the contest would be broadcast the following week. It meant that the choir would have to do the song justice to ensure that it would not be eliminated at the first semi-final stage.

He walked out of the central hall and strolled at a more leisurely pace towards the bus terminus thinking how he would break the news to his parents that the words that his father had written and the music that Jinky Jenkinson had composed might not be heard after all.

It was a gloomy return journey as the bus travelled along the New Town Road. He did not even look out the window as it passed The Liberty Arms such was the worry of the discovery of the terms printed on the banner stand. He alighted and made his way down the lane leading to the street where his parents lived. As he turned the corner Glen was curious when he viewed a taxi with its engine running outside the house.

His demeanour lightened somewhat when he viewed his Uncle Andy stepping out of the vehicle complete with overnight travelling case. After paying the driver Andy looked up the street and waited until his nephew joined him at the gates of the residence.

'I thought you were not coming until next week,' said Glen as he gave his uncle a warm embrace.

'I think you and your mum might need some extra support over the next week or so,' Andy replied. 'I've booked a few weeks holiday to stay with you.'

Andy Johnstone was a forty-five year old who kept himself in fine physical condition and his high cheekbone face still had the freshness of youth due to life of moderation in diet and only occasional alcohol imbibing at the weekends. Although only standing around five feet nine and a half he had been more than able to hold his own in the occasional rough and tumble in the city of Glasgow. Four years ago he had completed twenty years of service in the army but he had never divulged to Glen or anyone else the type of military work he was involved in even when the lad went to live with him in his flat in the Govan area.

He looked his nephew straight in the eye and asked. 'Where have you been this fine day?'

'Let's get inside and I'll explain when you get a cup of tea and I fill Mum in on the details,' Glen replied as he lifted his uncle's case and escorted him up to the house.

When they entered the hallway Anna ran up to them and threw her arms around her younger brother knowing full well she would need his additional support over the coming days as Derek's condition would probably continue to deteriorate.

As they sat at the kitchen table drinking cups of tea and eating cheese and tomato sandwiches Glen started to fill them in what he had discovered on the banner stand in Drumfast Central Hall.

'There is a chance that the song may not make the final ten to be broadcast next Wednesday,' he advised. 'I mean there must be dozens of tunes submitted by aspiring song writers all over the area.'

'If it doesn't go through it will just about finish Derek off,' added Anna. 'This is the final thing he wanted to tick off his bucket list.'

'Look Mum,' said Glen trying his best to reassure her. 'Jinky Jenkinson composed the tune and to me it sounded brilliant. Let's be positive and listen to the broadcast next week. What do you say Uncle Andy?'

'The lad is spot on,' replied Andy a smile breaking on his youthful face. 'We'll be there to support Derek when the show comes on the radio next Wednesday evening. Right! I'm going up to have a yarn with him.'

Anna and Glen looked at each other trying to reading other's minds. Thank goodness, they thought, for the extra support as it will be all hands to the pump over the coming days to ensure that the husband and father lived out his final days in peace and harmony. Their main hope would be that his final ambition would be fulfilled and the song would drift over the airwaves the following Wednesday.

CHAPTER TEN
****

The two days over the weekend seemed to pass at an untimely slow pace. It was a period of mixed emotions for the slower the pace of time passed by it meant that their loved one would be with them that little bit longer. However, the family were looking forward to the broadcast on Wednesday evening to discover if Derek's song would be an official entrant in the contest.

When Monday arrived it was obvious that the health of Glen's father was slowly going downhill. The visiting nurse was once again forced to increase the medication to keep the intense pain at bay. It seemed that only Derek's iron will was keeping his mind on track to discover if his last ambition was going to be fulfilled. There was a sense of dread that he might slip into a coma before hearing the song performed if indeed it was going to be an entrant into the final of the contest.

On Tuesday evening the Aunt Sarah arrived and when she entered the house she attempted to embrace Andy warmly who exchanged the greeting coldly as best he could under the circumstances. With those exchanges out of the way he moved into the living room to join Glen who was keeping well out of Sarah's way not wishing to be in her company.

Although Glen had no time for his aunt he always wondered what the dynamic was in the strained relationship with his aunt and uncle. He decided that the time was ripe to inquire what had happened all those years ago to force Andy to go and live elsewhere. There was a chance he could be rebuffed but he felt they had somewhat similar feelings about Sarah so he was curious to discover the full story.

'Andy, tell me to mind my own business if you wish,' he started off, 'but I always wondered why you left home at seventeen years of age and where Sarah came into the equation.'

His uncle sat for a moment in quiet contemplation and Glen at first wondered if he had spoken out of turn. Andy smiled and then issued a quiet word of warning to his nephew.

'If I tell you what happened do not let your mother know I have let you in on past family business,' he said. 'We have agreed to keep this in-house for all these years and the only reason I am going to tell you what happened then is that something similar has been done to you in more recent times.'

'What do you mean?' asked the now even more curious Glen.

Andy started off speaking quietly in case his two sisters should appear unexpectedly down the stairs from the bedroom. Glen leaned forward and his uncle started to relate softly the story which had been a burning issue in the family for the past thirty-seven years.

'As you know your Granny and Grandpa were killed in a car crash when the three of us were still pretty young. Sarah was the eldest and I was the youngest with your mother in between. I have to say for the first couple of years she brought us up pretty well under the circumstances. That was until she took up with a guy from the New Town Road called Billy Roberts. He was a ducker and diver who had never done a day's work in his life and she fell headlong in love with him.'

Glen interrupted Andy before he continued the story. 'I could never imagine Sarah being in love with anybody even when she was married to Uncle Charlie,' he said.

'Well, take it from me she fell for this smarmball hook line and sinker, said Andy. 'Roberts almost took up permanent residence in our house and he started to issue orders to your mum and me knowing full well that Sarah would back him up to keep on his good side.'

'Did you decide to leave when this started happening?' asked Glen.

'No, that was not the reason. There was no way I was going to leave your mother to be dominated by those two,' Andy continued. 'The three of us were working and every Friday in those days we got our pay in cash. When we took out our spending money for the week we each would put housekeeping money into a biscuit tin that was kept on a high shelf in the kitchen cupboard.

By the middle of the week I was usually almost broke but that was all right as long as I had enough to see me through until Friday pay day came around again. Anyway, there was a midweek floodlight cup match and United were playing City at their ground but I didn't have enough dough to get there and pay admission into the ground. Sarah and your mum were working overtime so I couldn't ask them to borrow the money from the tin. My mates were at the door calling for me to decide if I was going with them. I had to make a snap decision to take a few quid from the tin which I did after leaving an IOU to remind me to repay it back and it would let my sisters know what I had borrowed.'

'So you were able to get to the match and pay the money back on Friday?' asked Glen who was getting more and more curious to discover why his uncle had left the city to live in Glasgow. He could see a pained expression starting to come on to the face of Andy as he was about to relate the reason for his own exile from the city of his birth.

'Little did I know that Roberts was watching me from behind the kitchen door when I was borrowing the money. I didn't realise he was even in the house so he must have slipped in by the back door,' Andy continued. 'He always suspected that there was money hidden somewhere in the house and he knew I was anxious to accompany my friends to the game even though I was short of funds at that moment in time. That was fine until I got home from the match that evening and I was greeted with an angry bellow from Sarah and a worried look on your mum's face.'

Andy was about to continue when they heard the sound of Sarah and Anna talking as they descended the stairs. He put his forefinger to his lips and they pretended to watch television which they managed to switch on before the sisters entered the room. Glen was impatient to hear the end of the story so he attempted to conjure up a situation where his uncle and himself could continue with the narrative. Luckily his mother came to the rescue with a request.

'Glen could you go to the convenience store up the hill and get a bottle of honey, lemon and glycerine and a packet of cotton buds to wipe around your dad's lips,' said Anna. 'They are so badly cracked and dry and these will help to moisten them.'

'Do you want to come with me for the walk Uncle Andy?' he asked. 'You have hardly been out of the house these past few days.'

'No problem,' replied his uncle and he immediately went to the cupboard under the stairs where both his own overcoat and Glen's jacket were hanging up.

'Do you need anything else mum?' Glen asked. However, Anna shook her head signifying the only thing needed was the first items she had requested.

The two left the room without acknowledging the presence of Sarah with Glen especially hoping she would be gone by the time they returned with the items his mother had asked for. As soon as they got out of earshot in the street Andy continued his tale.

'As I said before, the stoney look and harsh greeting I received from Sarah told its own story. At first I thought it was because I had borrowed the money but there again I had left an IOU in the biscuit tin so really no harm was done. To my surprise and horror she lifted the tin out of the cupboard and almost pushed it up against my face. It was completely empty with no money to be seen.'

'What happened to the money?' asked Glen.

'It must have been taken by Billy Roberts as soon as I left for the match,' replied Andy as a frown entered his face. 'He must have emptied the tin and cleared off as soon as the coast was clear and then returned later in the evening as if it was the first time he had come into the house that night. There was no way I could persuade Sarah that I had nothing to do with the disappearance of the money.'

'What did mum have to say?' asked Glen. 'Did she not stick up for you?'

'At that time your mother was dominated by Sarah as we both were a lot younger than her,' said Andy. 'Roberts sat quietly in a corner of the kitchen and kept his mouth shut but he had plenty to say over the next couple of days as he bad mouthed me all over the New Town Road and beyond to deflect any suspicion away from himself.'

Glen could see the hurt in Andy's face as he was relating the events which had happened thirty-seven years before. It was obvious that there would be no going back to heal his relationship with his eldest sister. His nephew could now understand that the pain of isolation in another city was still raw in Andy just as it was within himself. The common denominator in the exile of the pair was Sarah and the people around her.

'What happened after that?' Glen inquired once again hoping that Andy would tie up any loose ends in the family history.

'I packed my bags and got out of there,' he continued. 'It almost broke your mother's heart but I couldn't take all the whispering and dirty looks from people in the district so I ended up in Glasgow. It was hard at first and I had to stay in a hostel but the small amount of back holiday pay I had on me was running out fast and there was a good chance I could have ended up on the streets.'

'Did that happen?' asked Glen who was really warming up to his uncle's life story.

'Thankfully not,' continued Andy. 'I was passing an army recruiting office one day on my way to the unemployment office and after reading the poster outside I went inside and signed up never thinking that it would give me a career and a good standard of living for the next twenty plus years.'

Andy had never spoken very often about his army career but Glen had discovered over the past three years that he was never short of finance so he realised that he must have a really good army pension as well as the wages he earned working as a guard for a security company in Glasgow. As they neared the convenience store Glen was anxious to get the answers to a final couple of questions he was about to pose to his uncle.

'What happened to the affair with Aunt Sarah and Billy Roberts?' he asked 'and when did Uncle Charlie come into the picture?'

'Apparently Roberts dumped her after a few years when he met another girl in one of the bars on the New Town Road,' said Andy. 'She took up almost immediately with Charlie on the rebound and married him when she was expecting your cousin Brian. The poor man had the life of a dog as she belittled him at every opportunity even though he was able to bring her to live in the house he owned outright when his mother died. There was talk that Brian's parentage was in doubt and your mum wrote to me stating that there was whispers that he was really Billy Robert's son. However, I'll take that with a pinch of salt. In the end Charlie had enough of playing second fiddle to the whims of Sarah and her spoiled brat Brian so he left to get out of the marriage.

'Where did he go to live?' asked Glen.

'I think it was somewhere in England,' replied Andy, 'but that is all I know. Charlie just cut himself off completely from Sarah and Brian. Can't say I blamed him and I hope he has a happier life wherever he might be. Anyway it turned out all right for your mum when she met and married big Derek. After two years you came along to complete their family.'

Glen had gotten more information in the last hour than he had been able to glean over his lifetime. His parents did not go in for tittle tattle so the family affairs of Sarah were never discussed either before or after his exile to Glasgow. Andy waited outside the shop while Glen picked the two items off the shelf and paid for them at the till.

The pair made their way back to the house mostly in silence with Andy only making another request to his nephew to keep what he had been told to himself. It was evident that even though he had been away for almost four decades he still adhered to the rule that family business was to be kept in-house.

To their immense relief as the turned the corner they were able to watch from the top of the street as Sarah left the house and walked away in the opposite direction towards the avenue where she lived. Andy and Glen gave each other a satisfied look knowing that they could relax for the rest of the evening with no toxic presence in the house. Glen packed his mother off to bed determined that he and Andy would take turns to see to the ill man's needs. It was vital that Derek should survive until Wednesday at least to discover if his song was about to be performed in the contest.

CHAPTER ELEVEN
****

The nurse left the house on the Wednesday morning of the song contest stating that the patient should only have one visitor at a time due to an increasingly lack of energy and too much talking would sap whatever strength he had left. This meant that the three people in the residence were between a rock and a hard place knowing that Jinky Jenkinson had promised to be there when the contest was broadcast that evening.

Glen was delegated to break the news to his father and he climbed the stairs very slowly mulling over in his mind what he was going to say. When he entered the room his father was propped up in four pillows with his eyes closed in peaceful repose. Glen panicked at first thinking his dad had passed away but heaved a mighty sigh of relief when Derek opened his eyes and smiled.

'How are you son?' he asked his voice seeming fainter than it had been the previous evening when Glen had sat with him.

'I'm fine dad,' Glen replied. 'I hope I did not disturb your sleep.'

'Not at all Glen, I'll be getting enough sleep where I'm going in the near future,' joked Derek.

The last sentence hit Glen like an arrow striking his heart. He had hoped his father would be with them for as long as possible but he now realised that Derek was reconciled to the fate that awaited him very soon. He could see that his last sentence had distressed Glen so he attempted to bring some levity into the proceedings.

'I'm not going anywhere soon until I hear that blasted song on the radio,' he quipped. 'I want you all to be here with me and hopefully it will be in the final ten.'

'That's just it dad,' said Glen breaking the news that the medical practitioner had dictated. 'The nurse says that there should be only one visitor at a time in the bedroom so you won't be exhausted.'

'Nonsense!' shouted Derek almost raising himself up from the pillows. 'What harm would it do for an hour or so to have the people who made this possible to be with me. No! This is my decision so I'll rest now and get my strength up for this evening. Tell your mother I have insisted and the nurse will never know the difference.'

Glen decided to leave the situation his father had dictated and took his leave to break the news to Anna and Andy who were having a cup of tea at the kitchen table.

'How did he take it?' asked his mother as she poured out a cup of tea for Glen when he took a seat at the table.

'He didn't!' replied Glen. 'He's determined that we are all there when the contest comes on air and no amount of persuasion will make him change his mind.'

Anna turned her attention to her brother. 'Andy could you go up and talk him around. It is only for his own good the advice that the nurse has given to us.'

Andy thought for a moment and then replied. 'Firstly if Glen could not get through to Derek I don't think I could make any difference. Secondly, you say it is for his own good. Well is it really? He wants family and his friend around him if, hopefully, the song will be broadcast tonight. So it is my humble opinion that we should be with him and that our presence would be for his own good. I don't think we should deny a dying man one of his last requests.'

Andy's summation swung it and Anna reluctantly agreed to allow the gathering around the bed just for the duration of the broadcast that evening. Glen almost took the stairs two steps at a time to break the good news to his father. Derek breathed a sigh of relief and closed his eyes to conserve his energy for the event he had been looking forward to over the past week - his song to be performed on the radio.

Around seven-thirty that evening the door bell rang and when Glen opened the door there stood Jinky Jenkinson resplendent in a bright yellow shirt underneath a genuine leather jacket. Glen tried to stifle a smile when he looked at him. He thought his father's old friend really looked the part of a showbiz type with his freshly laundered chinos and Nike trainers but this clothing was really only fit for someone many years younger. However, Jinky had a heart of gold and if that was the way he choose to dress so be it.

'Would you like a cup of tea Fred before we go up?' asked Anna as Jinky and Glen joined Andy and herself in the kitchen.

'That would be great Anna,' he replied. 'I need something to settle me down as I couldn't wait for my show to end this afternoon. I'm worried that I might have let Derek down.'

'For goodness sake Fred settle yourself down,' said Anna. 'Even if the song didn't get into the final ten entrants we still have the CD you recorded.'

'What with my voice yelling on it,' he laughed.

'Yes, with your voice yelling on it,' replied Anna laughingly as she poured out a cup of tea into a mug.

Jinky sipped his tea and although he was reassured by the attitude of the family there was still a sense of burning pride in his mind hoping that his professionalism would be recognised in the melody he had composed. The song would be some sort of legacy not only for himself but for his friend of years past.

The clock ticked by and when the time reached seven-fifty the four people climbed the stairs and entered the bedroom. To their surprise Derek was sitting upright and looked 'bright and bushy tailed' even though he still looked deathly pale. The thought of the song contest seemed to have removed any lethargy from his mind and body.

'Get the radio on Glen,' he gasped and Glen immediately adhered to his father's demand.

Anna was still worried that the presence of four people in the bedroom and the strain of listening to hear if his song would be broadcast over the air might exhaust her husband but this was his desire to have them around him. During the day Derek was forced to clear his throat continuously from the build up of sputum in his lungs and Anna was worried that this could be the first signs of pneumonia. But as the hour of the broadcast loomed he seemed to get a new lease of life and nothing would deter him from having the people closest around him to hear the contest.

The continuity announcer's voice coming from the radio speakers suddenly filled the bedroom. 'We now take you over to Drumfast Central Hall for the inaugural City of Music Song Contest.'

Derek leaned over to get as close to the radio without falling out of the bed. There was thunderous applause as the master of ceremonies kicked off the proceedings. Jinky gave a knowing smile as he knew the fellow who would introduce the songs. They worked at the same station but by no stretch of the imagination could they be called friends. This chap had been working at Drumfast FM since the station had started and he thought that the likes of Jinky were beneath contempt coming from the performing pop group area and shouldn't have been allowed near a microphone.

'Welcome, welcome everyone especially those of you listening on Drumfast FM.' The MC started off. 'Tonight you will be able to listen to ten songs specially chosen from a huge amount of entrants submitted over the past few weeks. We have four eminent judges who will give each song a number of marks and the audience here in the hall will also be able to cast their own votes electronically. Without further ado let's get going with the first song and, as with all the entrants, this will be performed by the Drumfast Gospel Choir and the Citybeats five-piece combo.'

The first song was belted out with the angelic voices of the choir booming over the internal speakers of the radio which sat on the chest of drawers beside the bed. It seemed quite good but nothing exceptional in Jinky's estimation. However, as one song after another was performed the gathering in the room was starting to get worried as the quality of the tunes seemed to be getting better and there was still no mention of 'This Land Is Not A Home'. Had Derek's song not made the top ten entrants?

Glen could see his father was getting downcast as they waited for the announcement of the penultimate song. A cry of jubilation echoed around the bedroom as the voice on the radio introduced the song they had been waiting for all evening - Derek's composition. They listened intently as the gospel choir performed the song brilliantly and did the song more than justice. When it was over Derek lay back against the pillows with a satisfied look on his gaunt face. To him the result of the contest was immaterial for he had heard his song performed professionally and that was all that mattered.

'Fred you've done me proud,' he said smiling at his old friend. 'Without you this would have not been possible.'

'Hold on a minute Derek,' replied Jinky, 'the results have still to be announced. It will be interesting to find out where the song ended up on the league table if you will excuse the football parlance.'

'It's OK Fred,' gasped Derek. 'All I ever wanted was to hear it performed professionally with music. I go to meet my maker happy with this tune ticked off the to-do list.'

Jinky's professional pride kicked in and he insisted that they listened to the programme until the results were announced. One by one the compere's voice ran through the names of the songs and their composers until he came to the top six. In sixth place there was still no mention of

LAST SONG FOR A RETURNING EXILE

Derek's song, no mention in fifth place until it came to the final three. By this time Anna and Glen were resigned to thinking the song was among the also rans and were feeling the most disappointment for Derek and indeed Fred Jenkinson.

Although Derek at first claimed to be unaffected by any result of the song contest he now seemed to be straining his ears to hear the final winner just to compare it with his own composition.

The voice of the master of ceremonies boomed out from the radio speaker. 'In third place is 'My Drumfast Love' by Erin Black, well done Erin. And now for the final two, there was only a few votes separating them and they are 'You're Here In My Arms' by Jim McLane and 'This Land Is Not a Home' by Derek McElroy.

When this was announced the bedroom at first went into bedlam with Anna placing her arms tenderly around Derek's shoulders and Glen and Jinky Jenkinson back slapping each other. When the excitement died down they listened intently to hear who the winner of the contest was going to be. Once again the compere took his time to build the atmosphere into a final exciting conclusion.

'In first place with the award of a silver trophy and five hundred pounds is 'You're Here In My Arms' by Jim McLane, congratulations Jim. And congratulations also to second place composer Derek McElroy who will also receive an engraved silver salver and two hundred and fifty pounds. The chairman of the judges will make the presentations to the winners. Although I believe Derek McElroy cannot be with us this evening so we will arrange to send the trophy and the cheque out to his home address as soon as possible.'

Jinky seemed crestfallen as he slumped into the chair as if he had lost a pound and found a penny. Derek once again assured him that his main ambition was to hear the song performed and to be the runner-up was indeed the icing on the cake.

'Look Fred, you have done a great job with the music,' added Anna. 'As far as I am concerned we all winners. Just look at Derek's face, he is as pleased as Punch.'

This seemed to settle Jinky down and after a moment he rose to leave thinking that all the excitement in the room was starting to exhaust the ill but very happy man lying on the bed.

'Derek my man, I'll come round tomorrow evening to visit you and see what kind of a trophy they have sent you,' he said with a smile on his tanned face. 'Get a good night's sleep and dream of winning the next contest for your new song.'

'Cheers mate,' muttered Derek and it was obvious that he was extremely tired due to the hub-bub surrounding him during the evening. He lifted his arm slowly and waved at his friend as he left the room. As Anna and Andy accompanied Fred down the stairs an eerie feeling entered the radio presenter's body with a chill running down his spine. He had encountered this feeling once before when he had left the hospital bed of his father who had been recovering from a major heart operation. On that fateful evening he had only reached home for an hour when he was sent for and when he reached the hospital once again he was told that his father had passed away suddenly.

When he said his goodbyes to Anna and her brother, Fred walked slowly down the garden path and stopped at the gates. He was hoping that the bad feeling he had in his bones was, maybe, just a coincidence because of Derek's condition. After staring up at the light coming from the front bedroom window for a moment he jumped into the car and drove off down the street.

CHAPTER TWELVE
****

When the room emptied Derek took the chance to have a one to one conversation with his son so he motioned Glen to come over closer to the bed. In a serious tone he started giving the young man some advice. Advice which surprised his son no end.

'Glen, you know that I have never been a vindictive person,' he started off, 'but there is something that I want you to do.'

'Tell me what it is Dad and I'll try do it,' Glen replied wondering what this request from his father entailed.

'You know how this is going to end,' Derek continued, 'and if things don't change regarding this exile your mother is going to be left on her own. Your Uncle Andy has his own life in Glasgow and I am worried how she will cope living a solitary life if you have to eventually leave the city as well after this is all over.'

'What about Aunt Sarah? I'm sure she will be calling round regularly,' Glen suggested.

'I really don't think it would be a good idea for her to be here too often,' said Derek. 'The next thing you'll find that son of her's will be here along with her and I don't want him about this house. Along with Bennet and McGaughey he is the main reason that we have lost the past three years together.'

Glen was anxious to discover what his dad required him to undertake to ensure his mother was secure and safe after his death. He didn't want to waste any more time in questioning his father in case Anna and Andy returned to the room so he let Derek continue the conversation without any further interruption.

'Son, as I said before, I hope that I have never been seen as a vindictive person,' he continued once again, 'but the situation we are in now will require drastic action, namely to avenge what has been done to you personally and which has affected this family as well. You will need to find some way of returning to Drumfast for good. Take it out on Bennet and McGaughey whatever way you think best son. This is with my blessing for if I had been able and on my feet in good health the pair of them would have been sorted out long ago.'

'Dad, rest assured if that is what you want I'll do whatever it takes to make this happen,' Glen replied.

He kissed his father on the head and prepared to leave the room when he heard his mother climbing the stairs. As usual she would take her turn and sit with her husband for another vigil through part of the night until the ill man fell asleep.

Glen lay for hours on his bed unable to get to sleep thinking up a number of scenarios how he could return to his home city. He dismissed the theories one by one as being completely impractical until the only feasible way out of the problem was to somehow get his hands on a copy of the document that Bennet had lodged with his solicitor. Not only would it land Bennet in serious trouble with his bosses but it had the capability of bringing down the whole organisation should it get into the hands of the law as it possibly contained names and addresses as well as the location of the safe houses where the drugs and money were hidden.

Just as he was drifting off to sleep he heard an agonising cry coming from the bedroom next to his room and it brought him back into full consciousness with a thud. He leaped out of bed and entered the bedroom to find his mother sobbing with her head on Derek's chest. As he lifted her gently back by the shoulders on to the chair Glen could sense the reason for her despair. There was no sign of life from his father and it was evident that he had passed away moments before. Glen cradled his mother in his arms as the tears from both of them dropped freely from their eyes.

'I will never be able to kiss him goodnight ever again,' cried Anna as she stared at the motionless body of her husband lying on the bed.

Andy, who was also wakened by the commotion, entered the room and immediately opened the bedroom window just above the bed where Derek was laid out.

'Why did you do that?' inquired Glen astonished at the first thing his uncle had done as he realised that his brother-in-law had died.

'Whether you believe it or not it's an old tradition that an open window allows the soul of the deceased to depart freely to join the souls of their loved ones,' explained Andy.

Anna nodded her head in agreement so Glen was satisfied that this was the done thing in these circumstances. The previous generation to his own still adhered to these age old principles so who was he to question them.

This situation was new to Glen so he was grateful that his Uncle Andy was there to take charge of things. The first thing he did was to phone an emergency doctor so that he could confirm the time of death and issue a death certificate. After an hour the practitioner arrived and undertook an examination of the body and issued the necessary documents before leaving.

Daylight was fast approaching when the doctor left and Glen and Andy sat in the kitchen to make a list of the things that needed to be done during the day. The first thing that needed to be undertaken was to contact a funeral director to take Derek's body away for preparation to lay him out in a casket. Anna and Glen could not look as their loved one was carried out in a black body bag to a funeral director's van parked outside the house. Andy had made sure his sister and nephew did not view this as it seemed a trifle undignified but necessary in these circumstances.

The day seemed to fly by as arrangements were made to remove the commode and medications from the bedroom. Sarah had arrived and proceeded to commence the catering arrangements for any callers who would arrive at the house to offer their condolences. This was one time that Glen and Andy were glad of her presence just as long as she didn't try to dominate the proceedings and bring her son Brian to the house. The three of them left her making sandwiches as they travelled to a local undertakers to make the arrangements for the funeral and choose a casket for Derek.

That evening Jinky, or to give him his proper name, Fred Jenkinson drew up at the McElroy residence unaware of the events of the previous night. When he rang the door bell a grim faced Glen opened the door.

'Well, how's the patient?' asked Jinky in complete ignorance of the proceedings of the previous hours.

'Fred he's gone,' replied Glen. 'He left us last night. I tried to get through to you but all I got was your answering machine and I didn't want to leave a message like that on it.'

'Oh my goodness,' gasped Fred. 'If I had known I would have come sooner.'

Glen led Fred into the living room where only Sarah, Anna and Andy were seated. He went over and embraced Anna and then sat down to hear what had transpired when his friend has died. Anna tried her best to hold back the tears as she explained her husband's last moments on earth to his shell shocked old friend.

'I decided to sit with him for a while until he went off to sleep,' she started off, 'but I nodded off only to be wakened by a rattle that seemed to be coming from his chest or his throat. I asked him, Derek are you all right, but he just grasped my hand tightly and gave a heavy sigh. That was when I knew he was gone and then Glen and Andy rushed into the room.'

'I had a strange feeling when I left here last night but I thought it was just because Derek had achieved his one remaining ambition of hearing his song performed,' said Fred not wishing to add that it was the same feeling that was in his mind when his own father had suddenly died.

'You would think that he hung on until he heard the song performed,' said Anna. 'At least he died happy with that ambition completed and his son by his side after all those years apart.'

Glen glanced over at Sarah and he could sense she was uncomfortable with Anna's last remark even though it was not completely directed at her. He thought, perhaps, there was an element of guilt in her demeanour as she rose and announced that it was time for her go home before it got too late.

Anna accompanied her to the door and when she returned to the living room she said, 'Sarah doesn't like to be out at night on her own.'

'Dear help any brave attacker who tries to take her on,' added Andy attempting to bring some levity into the gloom of the room.

After drinking a cup of tea and eating one of the sandwiches that Sarah had prepared earlier Jinky decided that he had outstayed his welcome and said that he could be contacted on his personal mobile phone to hear about the funeral arrangements for the following Monday. Anna insisted that he should be in the house the morning of the funeral to say his final goodbye to his friend as the coffin would be sitting in the living room.

Later in the evening Glen insisted that his mother should have an early night as she looked completely exhausted. She had done her duty in tending to her husband over the period when palliative care was needed to comfort him in the last stages of his life. The next day would have all the hallmarks of a traumatic one when the casket bearing the body of her husband arrived to lay in repose in the living room of the house he had worked so hard to buy.

Glen was surprised when he came down the stairs early the following morning to find his mother preparing breakfast in the kitchen.

'What are you playing at Mum?' he said as he sat the cereal bowls on the kitchen table. 'I could have done that. You were supposed to have a good rest before Dad comes home today.'

'I was only able to doze off in fits and starts so I need to be doing something to make sure things are right for later on today.' she replied.

Glen could detect the whiff of furniture polish combined with the smell of a sweet air spray so he realised that Anna had been up since early morning light. He didn't continue to admonish her for her early rising as this was probably one small way of dealing with her grief. His way of dealing with his own grief was one of anger due to the very short time he had been able to spend with his father in his last days.

The final words he had exchanged with his father kept running through his mind when Derek had said 'the situation we are in now will require drastic action, namely to avenge what has been done to you personally and which has affected this family as well. You will need to find some way of returning to Drumfast for good.' He had made a promise to his dying father and he was determined to carry out that request to the letter one way or another.

It may be a step too far to undertake this action on his own so he would probably need his Uncle Andy to be by his side when the time came to move into action.

The voice of his mother speaking to his uncle broke into Glen's thoughts as Andy entered the kitchen and sat down at the kitchen table trying to stifle a yawn.

'Some toast Andy?' she asked.

'That would be fine,' he replied and looking at Glen he added, 'when we get our breakfast we need to clear the settee away from the window to make room for the coffin.'

Although this last remark seemed a trifle cold Andy's time in the army had taught him to get things in order to suit any situation. Glen nodded his approval and when both looked over at Anna they could see the tears running down her face probably triggered by her brothers last remark.

Andy went over to her as she stood at the cooker and embraced her in his arms. At that moment he thought it would have been better to say nothing and just move the furniture when Anna went up to her bedroom to change for the day.

'Anna I am so sorry,' he apologised. 'Sometimes my mouth isn't in the same gear as my brain.'

'It's all right Andy I know you are just trying to help,' she sobbed. 'I'm going up to change out of my pyjamas. Just give me a shout if you need any help to move things about.'

Glen and Andy finished their breakfast and moved into the living room where they moved the three seater settee across the room to leave a space at the window where the casket would be placed.

Eventually everything was in order and the only thing now was to await the arrival of the funeral directors bearing the coffin with the body of Derek McElroy to lay in repose for the last few nights in his living room.

CHAPTER THIRTEEN
****

The black hearse drew up just before midday. Sarah had arrived an hour earlier and the four stood in the hallway attempting to support each other as the coffin bearing the remains of Derek entered his home. The undertaker's men placed the casket at the window in the space that Glen and Andy had provided and it would rest there for three days before going to the funeral home for a service of thanksgiving for the life of the deceased.

The lid of the coffin was placed against the wall of the room and once the undertaker's men had left the house the four people approached the casket to look at the body of Derek in peaceful repose. Anna stroked his face, then ran her hand across his auburn hair and stroked it into the way he always liked to style it in better days. Glen was trying his best to not let the emotion of the occasion get the better of him but when a tear from his mother's eyes dropped on to Derek's cheek he could hold back no longer. As Glen wept in his Uncle Andy's comforting arms Sarah stepped back not knowing how to react in the circumstances. So many years had passed since the death of her mother and father that it was hard for her to completely remember her emotions at that sad time.

After sitting in the living room just staring silently at the coffin for around half an hour they gathered themselves together. Anna went to the kitchen to make a cup of tea leaving Glen and Andy in the uncomfortable company of Sarah. It did not take long for the aunt to ask the question that had been haunting her over the past day.

'I was wondering have you organised the lifts of the coffin yet?' asked Sarah.

Glen immediately latched on to what she was hinting at and he was quick to disabuse her of any suggestion she might have regarding the pall bearers after the service.

'We are having just one lift when we leave the funeral church,' he said. 'Andy, myself, Fred Jenkinson and Barney from The Liberty Arms will take it from there and also carry it to the graveside.'

'That is ridiculous,' stormed an angry Sarah. 'Barney and Fred are not even relatives. My Brian should have been given one of the lifts, even the one at the cemetery.'

'Aunt Sarah, let's have a bit of truth here. You and I have never seen eye to eye,' replied Glen, 'but I want you to sit with us at the front of the church because of the help you have given my mother when I have been forced to live away. As far as Brian is concerned it was one of my father's final wishes that he didn't want him about the house so I presumed he wouldn't want your son carrying him to his final resting place.'

'So I take it he will not be allowed to sit at the front with the rest of the family?' she asked. 'At a time like this I think it is time to forgive and forget. Not that Brian has anything to be sorry for.'

'That is your opinion Sarah,' added Uncle Andy. 'You are one of the few people who believes that Brian had nothing to do with Glen's exile in Glasgow for the past three years. We know the true story. This young man has been robbed of the love and companionship of his mother and father during that time. He is entitled to be bitter about it.'

'Personally I wouldn't want him in the church,' said Glen forcefully, 'but that would be outside my control. However, I don't want him anywhere near us at the graveside when we commit my father to his final rest.'

Sarah rose up and just as Anna arrived with a tray bearing cups of tea and sandwiches the angry woman addressed her final comments to her sister before leaving the room.

'Anna. I am going now and I'm not sure if I will be back here before the funeral,' she said. 'I am also going to think things over if I will even go to the funeral. Your son is a very bitter young man.'

With that final riposte Sarah stormed out of the room leaving Anna bewildered and wondering what had been said in her absence. She sat the tray on the glass table in the middle of the room and slumped down on the settee thinking that this was all she needed whilst grieving the loss of her husband.

'What on earth happened when I was in the kitchen?' she asked looking over at Glen and Andy for some sort of explanation.

'She wanted to know who was taking the lift of the coffin,' said Andy. 'When Glen told her who the four were and that he didn't want Brian about the place, she blew her top.'

'I was hoping this could be avoided but there is nothing we can do now,' added Anna. 'We need peace to reign in this house for the next couple of days.

Over the period of Derek's laying in the house there was a steady stream of callers to offer their condolences to the family. Glen was amazed how popular his father really was as the sympathy cards from the locality and the people he had worked with piled up on the mantelpiece. The silver salver that Derek's song had won in the contest was delivered the day before the funeral plus a cheque for two hundred and fifty pounds. His trophy was at first placed on the mantelpiece in full view as it signified the last ambition which was fulfilled before he passed away.

At first Anna could not bear to even look at the trophy but Glen persuaded her to read the inscription engraved on it. Anna then realised that in receiving the award she was accepting it on behalf of her late husband. It was moved to a place of honour in the middle of the glass table to allow the growing number of sympathy cards to be placed on the mantelpiece..

The evening before the funeral was quiet in the home as the last callers departed just leaving the three members of the family to their thoughts. Just as they were preparing to sit down to spend a few hours with their loved one and have a deserved cup of tea a knock came to the door.

'Who could that be?' asked Anna. 'I thought the last of the callers had gone.'

'I'll go and see who it is,' said Andy. 'Hopefully it is somebody just leaving a card or a bunch of flowers or something like that.'

When he opened the door he was at a loss whether or not to admit the unfamiliar person standing there at this late hour. Nervously holding a card in her right hand was none other than Marlene, Glen's girlfriend from the past and now the wife of his cousin and nemesis Brian Wharton. Andy was unaware who she was as he had been long gone from the city and area before Marlene and Glen had become an item.

'I just want to leave this sympathy card with the family,' she said, her voice shaking slightly. 'If you could tell Glen and Anna how sorry I am for their loss I would be very grateful.'

'Thank you so much,' said Andy. 'Who can I say left this? Oh! I am so stupid it would say so on the card.'

Glen wondered why Andy was so long at the door and had just walked into the hall as Marlene was about to turn on her heel and return down the path. He had mixed feelings whether to call out to her and invite her inside but his mother had joined them and made the decision for him.

'Marlene, come in love,' she said. 'You have come all this distance so there is no way you are going to be left on the doorstep.'

'Thanks Anna but I'll not stay very long,' she replied.

They all moved into the living room and Marlene immediately walked over to the coffin and stood as if transfixed looking down at the body of the man who in happier times could have been her father-in-law. She then sat down opposite Glen and Andy while Anna did what she had been doing for the past number of days, namely making tea for visitors.

The one time love birds stared at each other waiting to see who would make the first remark. Finally it was Marlene who broke the silence.

'Derek looks very peaceful,' she remarked. 'At least he is out of pain now.'

'I suppose so,' replied Glen trying hard not to make the reply too dry. 'He battled really hard right to the end.'

As he kept looking at Marlene it was evident the past five years had not been kind to her. She seemed to have lost a lot of weight and her features appeared somewhat haggard. The once pretty face had all but disappeared. It seemed that marriage to Brian Wharton had taken its toll not only on her mind but in her body as well.

The atmosphere in the room had taken on a strange, slightly nervous feeling as if the two younger people sitting there looked like complete strangers. Thankfully Anna arrived with the tray containing four cups of tea and a pastry each for everyone and that broke the awkward feeling as everyone drank the tea and consumed the pastries.

'How is married life treating you?' asked Anna pretending to be completely ignorant of the state of Marlene and Brian's relationship.

'Oh! It has its ups and downs,' Marlene nervously replied looking over at Glen as if to indicate that she would someday wish him to take her away from the clutches of an uncaring husband.

'Ah well, that is what we all sign up for,' added Anna trying to add a little humour into the proceedings.

Marlene sat on for a few more awkward moments and then decided it was time to leave. She said she would walk to the phone box down the street and phone for a taxi to take her home to a presumably empty house. After going over to the coffin to have one last look at Derek she was accompanied to the door by Anna, Glen and Andy.

'Marlene you are quite welcome to attend the funeral tomorrow,' said Anna looking at Glen for his approval which he answered with an affirmative nod of his head.

'Thank you so much I'll try my best to attend and once again I am so sorry for your loss,' she replied and kissed Anna on the cheek.

'Glen, walk Marlene down to the phone box and wait there with her until the taxi arrives,' commanded his mother much to his consternation.

He gave Anna a kind of anguished look but proceeded to put on his coat for the one hundred yard journey to the phone box. There was no talk at all as the pair walked down the street and Marlene entered the box and phoned for the cab to pick her up outside it.

'They said it will be here in fifteen minutes,' she said eventually breaking the silence. 'I'll wait here until it comes. I should be all right here and I'm sure you'll want to get back to the house.'

'No. I will wait here with you until it arrives,' he gallantly replied. 'At this time of night the street is no place for a woman standing alone.'

It was a long time since a man, especially her husband, had given her any consideration of the type that Glen was giving her now. She looked into his eyes and the tears streamed down her face. He was at a loss what to do and placed his arm around her slim shoulders to give her some kind of comfort.

'Glen I am so sorry that I didn't wait for you,' she burst out crying, 'but your Aunt Sarah and my mother put so much pressure on me to marry Brian I was left with no alternative.'

Glen was struck into silence at this disclosure and was taken aback even more when she suddenly put her arms around his neck and attempted to kiss him just as they once had done in the past when they were a couple. He recovered his composure and gently held her away at arms length with his hands on her shoulders.

'Marlene this cannot be,' he said forcefully. 'It looks like you are unhappy with Brian and from what I can see he spends most of his time in The Liberty Arms with his mates and who else. Probably with the women who drink there. However, you are a married woman and at the moment I have to be very careful the way I operate when I am back here in Drumfast. I am on a very short lease and it takes one wrong move to get to the ears of Greg Bennet and I am out of here even before my dad's funeral.'

'I'm so sorry Glen but it's just that it is a lonely life living with a man who makes a living doing something that is a mystery to me,' she cried. 'Please, just ignore and forget what has just happened here.'

'No problem,' he replied. 'Marlene you must know how he gets his money without having to go out to work in a factory or a supermarket. He's doing what he always has done, dealing drugs.'

'I dare not ask,' she said. 'When I did accuse him of dealing I got a couple of slaps and was thrown against the wall and I was told in no uncertain terms to keep my mouth shut.'

Before the conversation could go on any further the taxi arrived earlier than had been expected and Glen helped Marlene into the back seat. As it drove off he could see her watching him standing there from the rear window of the vehicle. The animosity that he felt towards her had almost disappeared at that moment and he felt so sorry for the predicament she was now in. However, the hatred he felt for his cousin now increased twofold as he returned to the house after walking slowly thinking over what had been said in the brief conversation with his ex-girlfriend.

The thoughts of revenge on the people who had robbed him of life with his family had to be put on the back burner until his father's funeral was over. One of his father's last wishes was that he should get even with the perpetrators and he was determined to do so once they laid Derek to rest.

CHAPTER FOURTEEN
****

The sky was clear of clouds on the Monday morning of the funeral and there was no sign of rain. The three main mourners gazed into the coffin of their loved one to say their last personal goodbyes before the lid was placed on the casket for the journey to the funeral church. Glen and Anna kissed the body of Derek on the forehead while Andy stood back waiting to support one or both should grief overcome them. This was not required as both moved back beside him and watched with dignity as the undertakers carried Derek from his home for the last time.

After walking down the path to walk to the first funeral car they watched as the family wreath was placed on the top of the coffin before it was put in place in the hearse. Glen looked at his mother and he thought she looked so small at that moment dressed somberly in her black dress and coat. The pain in his own heart paled into insignificance compared with the loss his mother was enduring at the death of her partner in life. He placed his arm around her waist in a vain effort to comfort her as the back of the hearse was closed signifying the last private act the family would have before the more public acts of the service and committal at the cemetery.

Anna, Andy and Glen entered the car and it drove slowly behind the hearse along the street taking Derek on his last journey along that thoroughfare. The neighbours who were not attending the funeral stood silently as the cortege passed by and most of the men removed their caps as a sign of respect. When they arrived at the funeral church Barney and Fred Jenkinson were waiting outside to take their place as pallbearers along with Glen and Andy. Anna was shown inside to her seat at the front of the church by one of the funeral directors and she sat waiting alone to be joined by her son and brother once they completed their duties when they carried the coffin up the aisle of the church.

It was a short walk up the aisle of the packed church as the four men bore the coffin of Derek McElroy. The thought was running through Glen's mind that this was the worst and saddest walk he had ever undertaken and one he hoped that he would never have to take for a long time in the future. At the front of the church the funeral directors relieved the pallbearers and placed the coffin on two stands in preparation for the service to begin.

As Glen, Andy and the other two men were about to take their seats the door at the rear of the church opened and Aunt Sarah marched up the aisle with her head held high and took her place on a seat reserved for her beside Anna. He had mixed feelings about her presence but she had been a great support to his mother in his absence in Glasgow. These thoughts were put on the back burner as the minister commenced the funeral service by announcing the first hymn 'The Day Thou Gavest Lord Has Ended'. When the hymn ended he asked the congregation to bow their heads in prayer before announcing another piece of music.

When the singing of the twenty-third psalm, 'The Lord is my shepherd; I shall not want' ended, the minister said another prayer and then asked Fred Jenkinson to give an oration recalling his relationship with Derek over many years. At times he morphed into Jinky mode when he spoke of the funnier escapades they had undertaken in their youth. After he sat down he looked at Anna as she dabbed the tear from her eye with a white handkerchief. She nodded in appreciation to him before the minister said a final prayer. As the coffin was slowly transported down the aisle the sound of Derek's song 'This Land Is Not A Home' boomed out from a recording Fred had arranged to be played at the end of the service. His old friend had done him proud.

The main mourners shook hands with the many people milling around outside the church until the funeral director indicated that it was time to proceed to the cemetery. As the funeral car followed the hearse towards the graveyard the three of them and Sarah, who had joined them, sat in silence dreading the final committal of their loved one.

Glen, Andy, Barney and Fred carried the casket towards the freshly dug plot. Glen wished the short walk to the grave would last for ever as this would be the last time he would be in close contact with his father even remotely. However, other people were standing around the grave and the cold was starting to bite into their bones so a short committal was usual at this time. As the minister said a final prayer it was lowered gently into the grave with Anna placing a rose on top and Glen throwing soil into the grave in the time honoured tradition. As they were saying goodbye to the people gathered around the grave Glen looked up and to his extreme anger viewed Bennet, McGaughey and his cousin Brian standing below a tree some yards away viewing the proceedings.

He was about to rush over to completely eject them from the area but Andy who had also seen them held him back.

'Don't let this descend into a farce son,' he whispered. 'That is what they want you to do. I'll go over and see what they are doing here.'

Andy marched over to where the three were standing and immediately demanded why they had taken the trouble to come to the cemetery to view the funeral of a man who had no time for any of them.

'Look here,' Andy started off, 'I'm trying my best to keep that young man over there from sorting the three of you out. You would be better served by getting out of here pronto.'

'We're only here to support young Brian here,' said Bennet. 'He should have been part of this funeral.'

'Don't make me laugh,' replied Andy. 'Derek hadn't bothered with him for years and he would have turned in his grave if he thought this numpty had anything to do with his funeral.'

'Now look here I only wanted to pay my respects even from a distance,' interjected Brian. 'But I have been pushed out for no good reason.'

'And you know the reason why,' said Andy and as he was about to turn on his heel to join the rest of the mourners Bennet shouted out what was deemed to be a final demand.

'Tell that young glipe Glen McElroy his time is nearly up,' he warned. 'If he's not out of the city within the next couple of days we'll come looking for him if he doesn't report to me before then.'

'Is that so,' said Andy. 'Well you may not have to look very far. He may come looking for you before the couple of days are up.'

Bennet and McGaughey smiled at each other at the very suggestion of Glen taking revenge on them but Brian Wharton walked away a very worried young man. He knew a time could come when Glen would desire to get even with him for the hurt he had brought about to himself personally and his family in general.

Glen watched as the three hopped into Bennet's car and drove off. He was still seething at the temerity of them encroaching on the family saying a sacred goodbye to the head of the family. Andy put his arm around Glen's shoulder and led him away out of the earshot of his mother.

'Glen calm down son,' he spoke in reassuring terms. 'You time will come to get even with those galoots and it will be pretty soon if I have my way. Just let us get this day over with and then we'll think out our next move to bring those morons down.'

Andy's assuring words had the desired effect and Glen once again concentrated by supporting his mother in this, the saddest of days in the life of her family.

When the funeral tea at the hotel was over Anna, Glen and Andy left for home. Fred and Barney declined the invitation to come back for tea stating that the family needed some time to themselves. Sarah had left the cemetery in a huff after seeing her son standing well away from the committal service. She asked a neighbour to give her a lift home after declining an invitation to accompany Anna and the family to the hotel. It was obvious she was in complete denial of anything Brian had done and was oblivious that her son was still engaging in criminal activities across the murky underworld of Drumfast.

Andy had laid down a marker when he had issued a veiled threat to Bennet and McGaughey at the cemetery. He knew they would probably brush it aside thinking they were untouchable both from the long arm law and the upper echelons of the drug organisation. They possessed the threat of having documents in their solicitor's possession which would hang the leaders out to dry and henceforth straight into prison if anything should happen to his or McGaughey's person. Brian Wharton, however, knew he was vulnerable as he was only a foot soldier, albeit a valuable dealer of drugs on the streets of the district. At the moment his overriding fear was that Glen may come looking for him before he returned to Glasgow.

As the evening progressed Anna was exhausted and decided to have an early night leaving Glen and Andy sitting in the living room watching television. With the removal of the coffin the room was back to its normal set-up. Glen went to the living room door to ensure that his mother was well out of earshot as he and Andy started to plan their next move to exact retribution on the people who had ruined the last part of his life. It was one of his father's last wishes to get even with them and one he intended to carry out to the letter.

'The key to ensure you will be able to return home permanently is to get those documents from that crooked solicitor,' said Andy. 'We need to find out where he keeps them. They could be either in a safe in his office or in his home.'

'There's one person who could find out where the documents are kept,' replied Glen, 'and that's our pal Barney. He has access to Bennet's office and he could do a bit of a hoke around in there when they are not about to see if he can find out where the papers are stashed.'

'I'd better not go near the bar and the same goes for you too Andy,' said Glen. 'I've got his phone number so I'll give him a buzz tonight. He should get home after work in the bar around twelve midnight.'

'If he knows where the documents are hidden we will need to act quickly,' added Andy. 'We only have only around two days to break into the office or the solicitor's house and then hand the papers over to the police.'

'When the time comes on the day I'm supposed to leave I want you to hold on to the documents until I am leaving The Liberty Arms and to pretend that I am going to the train station,' said Glen. 'There is something I want to do before you hand them over to the cops.'

'And what's that?' asked Andy.

'You'll find out when the time comes,' replied Glen wishing to keep his intended action to himself in case his uncle tried to persuade him otherwise.

The pair of them watched television until it was time for Glen to put on his coat and walk down to the phone box further down the street. He inserted the requisite number of coins into the box and rang Barney's home number. Thankfully there was an answer on the other line and the familiar voice spoke.

'Hello, Barney Elliott speaking,' it said. 'How can I help you?'

'Barney, it's Glen here,' he answered. 'Sorry to ring you at this late hour but I need your help badly.'

'I'll help you if I can son. What would you need me to do?' Barney asked.

'All I need is a bit of info where the documents that Bennet has hidden are being kept,' Glen replied.

There was silence on the other end of the line for a moment and Glen wondered if Barney was reluctant to divulge the information in case he would lose his job at The Liberty Arms in the process. He need not have worried as Barney spoke once again in measured terms down the line.

'I'm not completely certain where they are hidden but it would be sensible for them to be in a safe in the solicitor's office,' asserted Barney. 'It would be too dangerous for documents like this to be kept in a house where it could be easily broken into.'

'Do you know where these offices are?' asked Glen. 'What's the name of the solicitors?'

'They are in a building on the other side of the city well away from this district,' said Barney. 'Reggat Road is the name I had overheard McGaughey and Bennet mentioning a couple of times when I would bring their coffee into the office in the afternoon. I think their solicitor is Benny Farr. He's almost as crooked as they are.'

'Thanks for this Barney, I'll let you get up to bed now,' Glen said.

'Just before you go lad,' added Barney. 'Let me give you a word of warning. You can be sure that place will be alarmed to the hilt and the safe could be one of a most state of the art type available. Benny Farr holds a load of stuff that could sink a regiment of narcotics organisations. Just be very careful.'

'If that's the case why has he not been raided by the police?' asked Glen. 'Surely they must have some suspicion what he is about.'

'Farr is virtually untouchable,' explained Barney. 'He is a member of a couple of clubs that are frequented by the area police commander and inspectors of that district of the city. So you see, it is a case of the old boy network at play here. As I said before Glen, be very careful what you plan to do.'

'I will. Goodnight Barney, thanks for this,' and with this final remark Glen hung up.

He almost sprinted up the street and once in the door of the house he immediately filled Andy in with the information that Barney had imparted to him. He was disappointed that his uncle did not seem too excited at what he had told him. Andy sat for a moment in deep thought and then gave his opinion, at first playing a sort of devil's advocate.

'If these offices are on the other side of the city taking buses will be no use,' he stated. Hopping on public transport is no way of making a quick getaway if we are discovered. This looks like a lost cause Glen. I could disable the alarm easily enough and maybe crack the safe but getting there is a major obstacle.'

'I thought it would be the other way around,' said Glen. 'How is it easy to disarm the alarm and open the safe when transportation would be so hard to get to the offices?'

'Maybe there could be one way around this,' suggested Andy. 'We could hire a car and that would solve the transportaion problem. Tell you what, I'll get my driving license out of the case and rent a motor tomorrow morning. I'll need to get into the city centre to buy something else as well.'

'Let me know what this will cost and I'll get you the money when you get back,' said Glen.

'Don't worry about that,' replied Andy. 'The main thing we will have do tomorrow night is to keep your mum in the dark. If she thought we were doing a break-in she would go spare so we will say we are going out for a night on the town.'

'Well there would be an element of truth about that,' laughed Glen. 'We are going out for a night on the town but for a different reason.'

'Correct,' said Andy. 'I think it's time we got some shut-eye. We have a big day tomorrow to make things right for this family.'

With these final words they turned out the lights and climbed the stairs. Glen lay for a while and pondered how his uncle would disable the alarm and break into the safe. It all depended how modern the systems were at Farr's offices. He hoped that Barney was wrong regarding the security aspects of the premises. Perhaps the solicitor was so sure he was exempt to any danger from the law due to his friendship with some area officers that he had not bothered to update his security and he knew the drugs organisation was unaware of the place where the documents were hidden. To leave a false trail Farr had spread rumours around the district that the documents were lodged in a bank somewhere in the south of England.

That was something that he and Andy would discover once they arrived at the offices the following evening. Glen drifted off to sleep content that things were on the move to allow him to come home from exile once and for all.

CHAPTER FIFTEEN
****

Glen wakened the next morning to the sound of Andy whistling as he washed and shaved in the bathroom adjacent to his bedroom on the landing. He waited until his uncle had finished his ablutions and took his turn in the bathroom. Anna had been up and about for some time before the pair of them had risen and he could hear her preparing the breakfast and starting to converse with Andy down below in the kitchen.

When he came down and entered the kitchen he hugged his mother and inquired how she was feeling. Under the circumstances she indicated that she was fine but he knew her heart was breaking at the loss of her husband and best friend. Glen could only admire her courage as Anna attempted to undertake some sort of semblance of normal living the day after Derek's funeral.

'What are you up to today Andy?' she asked her brother as she poured out cups of tea for the three of them.

'I'm thinking of heading into the city centre and hiring a car,' he replied.

'Why would you want to do that?' she inquired. 'Do you think it will be worth the expense for all the time you may be here before heading home to Glasgow?'

'Take it from me Sis it will be worthwhile,' he said with a smirk on his face as he looked over at Glen and winked. 'I was thinking we could go for a couple of trips in it, maybe down to the lakes. It would do you good to get out of the house for a while.'

'If you think so,' she said and left the conversation at that.

Glen could only smile into himself. There was no doubt his Uncle Andy could talk himself out of any situation. It was then that he wondered what Andy had done during his time in the Army. In all the three years he had lived with him in Glasgow he would never divulge what his role was in the forces. When Glen had pushed him for a disclosure all he would reveal that he was in a communications unit. He always suspected that there was more to Andy's service in the Army than he would admit but hoped that someday he would find out what his uncle had got up to during those years in the service.

As Andy was leaving the house to catch a bus into the city centre he noticed an envelope lying underneath the letter box in the hallway. Scribbled on the front was the words 'FAO Glen McElroy'. He immediately brought it into the kitchen and handed it to Glen as he munched on a piece of toast. Andy decided to wait until his nephew divulged the contents of the note within the envelope.

'Hope this is not a love letter from some girl hoping to get a date,' he joked.

When Glen started reading the look on his face told Andy that this was certainly not the case. A worried look encompassed Anna's face when Glen threw the note on to the kitchen table in anger.

'What did it say?' asked Andy now wishing he had not cracked the joke beforehand.

'I've two days to get out of the city,' Glen replied. 'They were fly enough not to sign it in case I went to the police but it is obvious where it came from.'

'It is a downright cheek to come up to my door at a time like this and post something like that through the letterbox,' Anna said angrily. 'Is there nothing we can do about this before they force Glen to leave?'

'Don't worry Anna,' said Andy soothingly, 'we'll work something out over the next couple of days. Now I'm off into town,'

With another wink towards Glen he left the kitchen and this time he was able to leave on the errand to catch the bus into Drumfast city centre. Hopefully he would not be forced to take public transport on the return journey as with a bit of luck he would be in possession of a hire car.

It seemed like an eternity before Andy returned from the city centre. However, later that morning the front door opened and a smiling Andy motioned Anna and Glen to come outside to view a shiny white Ford Anglia parked on the road close to the pavement. He opened the door to allow the pair to examine the upholstery and they were suitably impressed.

'Get inside and I'll take you for a spin around the district,' he offered Anna and Glen.

However, Anna declined the offer and indicated that it was close to lunchtime so she would start preparing the meal in readiness for the men's return from testing out the motor. As they drove around the corner of the street Andy pulled in and parked outside the convenience store where they had bought some items the night before Derek had passed away.

Glen watched as his uncle got out of the vehicle and opened the boot before returning with a large brown paper bag which at first did not look very heavy. Andy immediately pulled out a two foot long heavy duty pair of carbon steel wire cutters and handed it to Glen who was curious why his uncle had bought them. There was no explanation forthcoming as Andy once again delved into the bag and pulled out a doctors stethoscope.

'What are these for?' Are you going to pull teeth and then check if the patient is still breathing?' Glen joked.

Andy's face took on a serious look. 'Do you remember what I said last night?' he said. 'That the main problem would be the transport.'

'Yes,' replied Glen.

'Well we now have the transport and these two beauties are the keys to getting our hands on the documents in Farr's office.' Andy replied and taking the wire cutters from Glen he added. 'If we need to cut any wires or chains these boys will do the job and the scope will enable me to listen to the clicks when I get the combination to crack the safe.'

'What did you do in the army?' asked Glen hoping that he could get the information that had evaded him for the past three years.

'That I cannot say,' replied Andy. 'All I can say is that I can't disclose anything I have done in the past under the Office Secrets Act. Let's leave it at that.'

With that snippet of information coming from his uncle Glen reckoned Andy had worked undercover in his time in the army. This would explain why he was so confident of breaking into the solicitor's office and opening the safe containing the telling documents. The anger that Glen had felt earlier in the morning after receiving the warning note had subsided as the end game was now in sight one way or another. But only if they were successful in getting their hands on the documents. If they were unsuccessful in this mission he was determined to wreak revenge on his tormentors one way or another.

Andy placed the wire cutters and the stethoscope back into the brown paper bag and put it back into the boot of the Ford. They sat in silence as Andy drove the short distance back to the house and parked the car outside close to the pavement. Glen was in a sunnier mood as the entered the house to find Anna finishing off the preparation of lunch.

'Well what did you think of the car Glen?' she asked.

'It'll do the job fine,' he replied as Andy's eyes opened wide in shock hoping Anna would not take the remark literally.

'It drives well,' Andy added, attempting to reinforce the fact that Glen was referring to the mechanics of the vehicle.

'Good!' said Anna and to their relief she poured out cups of tea to continue lunch.

All the two intended cat burglars could do was to wait for darkness to descend and leave on their presumed night out to a club in the city centre. They would be forced to leave Anna unaware of the true purpose of their trip into the cold night to find the means of Glen's release from three years of agonising exile.

CHAPTER SIXTEEN
****

Half past eight eventually arrived and Glen and Andy dressed themselves in smart and casual apparel as if they were going on a night out. Before they left the house Anna issued some advice and a warning to the pair.

'I think you should have taken a taxi,' she said. 'You wouldn't have had to worry about drinking and driving. Just be very careful, the police are cracking down on drivers who are over the limit.'

'I'll park the motor in a car park if I go over the limit,' replied Andy, 'but I intend to only have a shandy so we should be all right.'

Glen knew that their sobriety would be confirmed as having a drink was the last thing on their minds. Clear heads were the order of the day when they would attempt to break into the premises of Bennet's bent solicitor Benny Farr.

Just before they entered the car to leave for the other side of the city a figure jumped out of his car further down the street and hurried to catch them before they drove off. When he came up close it was none other than Fred Jenkinson or Jinky as he was known in local entertainment circles.

'Hi Fred,' said Glen. 'What are you doing around here at this time of night?'

'I'm just back from doing an early disco in The Liberty Arms,' he disclosed. 'Barney took me to the side to tell me what you are trying to do. He asked me to warn you that he discovered that the documents are not in Farr's offices in Reggat Road.'

'Then where are they?' asked Andy.

'Apparently Barney had overheard Bennet and McGaughey talking about an old spinning mill in Shedland Close. It had been converted into different types of offices and workshops a few years ago and Farr has a place there where nobody would think he keeps important stuff. Just be very careful there's probably twenty four hour security about the place.'

'Look Fred thanks for this info,' said Glen. 'You and Barney have been good friends to us and when this is all over one way or another I'll try to repay you in some way.'

'The best way you can repay us is getting that dirt off the streets,' replied Fred. 'And I mean dirt in both instances, Bennet, McGaughey, your cousin and the drugs they pedal.'

Fred placed the edge of his hand to his forehead and waved it in a form of salute. With that he strolled down the street, hopped into his car and made a three point turn before driving away towards the New Town Road.

Andy and Glen decided that it made no difference where they needed to break into. The only difference was that there might be the possibility of security guards patrolling in such a large establishment. They would have to plan their entrance 'on the hoof' when they arrived there. Glen hoped that Andy had encountered something similar when he was an undercover operative in the army and would know how to counteract any problem or persons that could block their way.

Before they drove off Andy asked Glen if there was any tools in the wooden shed at the rear of the house. Glen was unsure but indicated that the shed was kept unlocked as the lock was stiff and his mother had not the strength to force it open when she needed access. Should Anna come out and ask what he was doing there Andy decided to say that he needed a screwdriver in case he needed to prise open the hub caps of the car in case of a puncture.

In the event Anna was unaware of his presence at the shed and he arrived back at the car brandishing a small screwdriver, a piece of thick wire, an eighteen inch crowbar and a torch. Just the thing to prise open a stiff window or workshop door. He once again opened the door of the car boot and popped the crowbar and the other items into the big brown paper bag.

'Let's get out of here before your Mum comes out and asked why we are still here,' said Andy as he entered the car and slipped the stick into first gear. They moved off down the street towards the city centre and onward towards their destination at Shetland Close.

As they entered the opposite side of the city Andy was forced to stop the car to get directions to Shetland Close. Glen asked a passerby where the mill was situated and the man gave him the general direction around a mile up the road in the distance.

The converted mill was an imposing edifice and it was shrouded in darkness as no work was undertaken there on late evenings. Glen and Andy exited the vehicle which they parked down the road some distance from the entrance to the mill. When he opened the boot Andy stuffed the crowbar into the belt of his trousers and the stethoscope into his coat pocket while Glen did likewise with the wire cutters, the small screwdriver, the thick wire and the torch. The tooled up pair moved to the side of the entrance and watched as the two security men started their tour around the huge building.

The main problem was finding where Benny Farr had his rented office/workshop in the building. There was a sign just inside the entrance gates so Andy and Glen waited until the security men walked out of sight. As they scanned down the notice board there was no mention of Farr anywhere on the list. It was only when Glen noticed a name that was unusual he started to put two and two together. Halfway down the list was a company named Rafneb Associates Limited and when the first name of the company was reversed it would spell benfar. So this was how Benny Farr kept the documents well out of reach in a little known office/workshop numbered one hundred and fifty-two.

There was an added problem that the premises were on the first floor. It would be too risky to jemmy the main door as this would be one of the first things the guards would always check on their rounds. They moved outside the gates once again and Andy watched their movements to monitor the length of time it took for the security men to complete their circuit of the big building. He reckoned twenty minutes and hoped that they might enter their hut which was situated half way along the building for a welcome cup of tea once a couple of rounds had been completed.

Looking at the layout of the place Andy decided that the safest place of entry was at the narrow end of the building just opposite to where they were standing. That area was in darkness and was just the ideal spot for a covert operation such as this. So it was a matter of patiently waiting until the security men either started their next round or entered the hut for the well deserved refreshments.

After the third round of circling the building the men entered the hut and closed the door to shield them from the night time chill.

'Right, let's go, it's now or never,' whispered Andy. 'By the time they finish their tea or whatever and go on another round we should be inside the building.'

When they reached the side of the mill Glen opened his coat and brought out the wire cutters and torch while Andy pulled out the crowbar from the belt around his waist. From the pocket of his coat he placed the stethoscope around his neck and to Glen's surprise he produced another small piece of heavy wire from his inside pocket.

'Something I learned in the scouts,' he whispered. 'Be prepared.'

He aimed the beam of the torch around the window to determine how it was locked. To his delight it was secured by a lockable handle at the side. It was evident that these were of a more modern type installed when the mill was converted to workshops. Andy knew that the window would need to be forced open with the crowbar. He motioned Glen to peep around the corner to ensure the men in the hut did not become aware of their presence should there be any noise when the window was forced open.

Glen could hear the faint sound of music coming from the direction of the hut. The security men seemed to like a bit of entertainment as they enjoyed their tea or coffee. He was startled when he heard the creak of the window being forced open and kept looking across at the hut to see if the noise had alerted the occupants inside it. There was no reaction from that quarter so he returned to see Andy climbing through the window and motioning him to follow suit. His uncle closed the window and pulled the handle down to hopefully hide the forced breakage to make it look as if it had never been opened.

Once both of them were inside the building they walked along a narrow corridor making sure the light from the torch was directed downwards in case it was seen from the outside. They came upon a lift but decided that the noise of the elevator rising might alert the security men if they had finished their tea in the hut.

Luckily there was a flight of stairs close by and the pair of them vaulted upwards two at a time.

When they reached a landing on the first floor to Glen's dismay there was a locked door leading to the corridor where they hoped Farr's office/workshop was situated. However, Andy was not to be deterred from gaining access to the corridor.

'Where's that small screwdriver you brought out from the shed at home?' asked Andy.

'It's in my pocket,' replied Glen.

'Give it here,' demanded his uncle. 'I'm going to show you something I learned in the army training school when we were locked out of the barracks after a night out on the tiles.'

The lock on the door was one of the old Victorian ironmongery type which had been in situ since the days when cotton was spun in the mill. Glen held the torch while Andy inserted the small screwdriver into the key orifice. He then wriggled the fine shaft up and down and from side to side with the heavy wire for what seemed to be interminable time until they heard the lock move into place and he moved the bolt backwards before pulling the handle downwards. Glen shone the beam at Andy as he stood up and he could see a broad grin enveloping the face of his uncle as he opened the heavy door.

'I told you my time in the scouts was not wasted,' Andy laughed.

'The only thing is you didn't learn to do in the scouts was picking locks,' replied the smiling Glen. His estimation of his uncle had gone up even more at that moment.

'Right let's find this place where Farr hides all his goodies,' commanded Andy. 'What was the number, one hundred and fifty-two if I remember correctly.'

'That's the one,' said Glen as they moved along the corridor shining the beam of the torch at the numbers on the doors. It was a long corridor and when they came upon one hundred and fifty-one they knew they had hit the jackpot. Their objective would be next door. To their surprise there was no number or name of the company on the door. Was Benny Farr making it as difficult as possible for anyone to trace this hideout? Tonight, in this case, it was completely unsuccessful.

CHAPTER SEVENTEEN
****

The windows of the rental were blacked out and when Glen shone the torchlight down the wall beside the door he could see what looked like a telephone wire leading inside the workshop towards the top of the door. He ran his hand up the wire to confirm that it could possibly lead to an alarm above the door frame. It meant that once the door would open the alarm could be tripped giving only around thirty seconds grace to allow the occupant time to switch it off.

Glen and Andy hadn't the knowledge of the location of a disarming switch inside the premises so it was a matter of brute force and ignorance to cut the telephone wire and either force open the door or better still repeat picking the lock which was the Victorian ironmongery type in common with the one at the end of the corridor.

'Give me the wire cutters and shine the torch towards the bottom of the wire just where it enters into the skirting board,' said Andy.

'Why are you going to cut it down there?' asked Glen.

'The wire is stapled tight against the wall,' he explained. 'If I cut it at the bottom it will be less noticeable when somebody comes along past it in the morning. Only Farr will realise it has been disabled when he decides to come here in the future and opens the door.'

A swift incision was made with the wire cutters and the line was cut. They listened for a moment in case the alarm went off but to their relief there was silence. It looked like the alarm was very basic and not the sophisticated type that Barney had feared. Andy whispered that he thought that it was perhaps a dummy alarm such was the confidence that Benny Farr had in concealing the whereabouts of the incriminating documents.

Andy once again went about his work with the piece of heavy wire and screwdriver to started to pick the lock with expert precision. Just as before, within a minute, the bolt was pushed back. He pulled the handle and gingerly pushed the door open just in case there was some sort of extra security apparatus powered by batteries. To their immense relief silence once again prevailed and they entered shining the torch around the room to discover the layout of the place and the location of a safe where the documents could be hidden.

The only items on view in the workshop was a battered looking leather armchair sitting behind an old wooden desk which was hosting an ancient looking telephone. Two wooden chairs placed at the front of the desk looked to have also seen better days. Obviously this place was only used for occasional clandestine gatherings involving Farr, Bennet and McGaughey when important meetings which would have taken place in The Liberty Arms could be vulnerable to prying eyes and listening ears.

The pair had been expecting to see a safe sitting on the dusty floor of the office/workshop but there was nothing else in view. The thought came into Glen's mind that Barney had been fed a curved ball and maybe Bennet had suspected him of passing on information. It was only when he aimed the torch around the rental that the reflection on a huge ornamental mirror hanging on the opposite wall shone back at him. He nudged Andy and his uncle moved over to investigate if the mirror was only there for decoration purposes or maybe the document possibly taped behind it. On second thoughts Andy decided that this was a non starter. Farr and Bennet were too shrewd to leave such damning information out in the open.

The mirror was hanging on a heavy chain attached to a bracket which was screwed securely into the brick wall. Andy, at first, attempted to lift it off the wall but the weight seemed too heavy for one person to undertake. Glen sat the torch down on the floor and with a bit of a herculean effort both of them were able to place it down on the office floor. He lifted the torch and shone it on the area of the wall which had been covered by the mirror only to discover there was nothing but bricks staring back at them. However, Andy motioned him to aim the beam of the torch closer to the area and he discovered that the top part of the brick area covered by the mirror had no cement between each row.

'Give me the crow bar Glen,' he commanded. 'This could be a dummy part of this wall.'

Andy prised the flat end of the crow bar between the crevice at the top of the rows and he was able to loosen one of the bricks which Glen caught before it would fall and smash onto the floor. Once one was displaced it was an easy job to dislodge and pile the remainder of the bricks on the floor. Lo and behold the safe they had been searching for was revealed and it was built into the cavity wall. The pair smiled at each other in immense relief knowing that this venture had not turned out to be a fool's errand.

With the stethoscope around his neck Andy immediately set about cracking the safe. From previous experience he immediately recognised that this smaller safe was one of the three wheel type. Placing the instrument against the door of the safe close to the combination lock to find the most audible location he went to work rotating the dial in an anti clockwise direction hoping to hear a faint click as the lever dropped into the notch on the wheel inside the safe mechanism. Each time he was successful he asked Glen to remember the number and after almost an hour he had the three number combination to open the safe.

'Give me the combination Glen,' he asked. 'I have been concentrating so much on getting each number I've forgotten the order of them.'

'Twenty-three, fifteen and thirty-one,' said Glen as he looked on expectantly for the safe to be opened.

From the light emitting from the torch Andy moved the knob of the safe backward and forward until he had located all three numbers. He turned the handle and to the delight of the pair the door of the safe opened. Glen shone the torch inside and stared in amazement at the rows of bank notes neatly piled in what looked like amounts of one thousand pounds. They looked ready to be possibly laundered by some shifty company in England or maybe by a ghost company on the continent of Europe. Sitting on top of the money was a A4 brown manilla envelope which they hoped would contain the document they had come here to take away.

Glen eagerly pulled it out of the safe, opened it up and Andy shone the torch on the paper as Glen read the contents. His eyes lit up as he read the first page of the deposition naming the leaders of the drugs organisation, their hidden addresses and where their finances were held in offshore accounts namely in Mauritius and Belize. This information could blow the whole cartel out of the water and was confirmation why Greg Bennet was allowed to act almost independently of the organisation.

On a second page was the names of the lower ranks namely the street dealers and to Glen's amusement and extreme satisfaction the name of Brian Wharton almost jumped out of the page. At the bottom was Greg Bennet's signature and it was witnessed by Eddie McGaughey.

'I'd love to see Aunt Sarah's face when the cops come knocking on Brian's door and they trail her golden boy away,' he laughed.

Andy was starting to get worried about the time they had been in the building. His army training kicked in once again and it told him that they needed to get out of there in case the security men undertook an inside inspection.

'Right, I'll close the safe and we'll have to replace the bricks in the same formation they were in before,' he said.

They closed the safe and quickly replaced the rows of bricks and with a bit of effort both lifted the heavy mirror back onto the wall hanging it once again by the chain attached to the bracket. Glen replaced the document into the envelope and kissed it before folding it in two and tucking it into the inside pocket of his coat. He would be able to read and digest it in more detail once they arrived home after they escaped from the clutches of the security men in the mill.

Just as they were about to exit the workshop they were alerted by the noise of the door at the far end of the corridor being opened and then shut once again with a loud echo due to the emptiness of the place. Glen peeped out and could see the beam of a large torch shining back and forth on each door as the person walked slowly along the long corridor. To their consternation it was one of the security men doing his internal rounds in this part of the building. Every now and again he would give a cursory pull at the door handles to ensure that the rooms were locked before moving on to the next one.

Glen quietly closed the door and whispered to his uncle. 'If he decides to try this door handle we will be rumbled. I don't really want to attack or injure the man as he's just doing his job.'

'Quickly, shine the torch on the door lock,' commanded Andy.

He laid the crow bar gently down on the floor and proceeded to work at the lock with the length of wire and the small screwdriver. The security guard was getting ever closer but was far enough down the corridor to enable Andy to thankfully slide the bolt into place once again before he came close to their hiding place.

'I hope he doesn't notice that the telephone wire is cut if he shines the torch downwards,' whispered Glen.

'I cut it neatly right on the skirting board,' replied Andy. 'With a bit of luck he'll just concentrate on the door handle. Even so, he'll never dream of anybody being inside here.'

The noise of footsteps on the tiled floor came ever closer and stopped outside the door. Glen had switched the beam of the torch off in case any light protruded through the narrow gap at the bottom of the door. The door handle moved downwards and they could hear the grunt outside as the man pushed against the door to ensure that it was securely locked. The handle moved up again into its proper place and they listened intently as the noise of the footsteps faded into the distance and the door at the end of the corridor clanged shut.

Andy once again placed the wire and screwdriver into the lock and as he was now familiar with its workings he had the bolt moved back quickly into the open position. They waited for a few moments to allow time for the security man to get far enough away to allow them to make their escape from that part of the building. Glen switched the torch off and the two of them walked quickly down the corridor to be met with another obstacle - the main door out of the corridor was once again locked.

As he had done before Glen shone the torch beam on to the lock to enable Andy to once again unlock the door. It was taking him longer this time as he moved the heavy wire and the small screwdriver back and forth in the lock.

'What's the problem Andy?' he asked.

'I think the stupid man has left the key in the lock on the other side,' his uncle frustratedly replied. 'It's blocking the access to the bolt mechanism.If we don't do something he will probably twig on that he has left the keys hanging there'

'We could be stuck here until the morning unless there is another door at the opposite end of the corridor,' advised Glen.

'That's our only option,' replied Andy. 'With a bit of luck it will have the same type of lock as this one.

The pair sprinted along the corridor and luckily enough it was a similar type of door and locking mechanism blocking their way out of the mill. Andy once again got to work and this time he was able to slide the bolt into the open position. As they were now at a different location in the mill the problem now was to find the route back to the window Andy had prised open earlier to allow them to once again exit on to the courtyard. As they descended the stairs and moved about in the darkness it was like trying to get out of a maze as corridors in the old Victorian mill abounded left right and centre.

The time was ticking away and it took three attempts before one of the corridors led them to a window situated at the opposite end of the building from where they had first entered. Glen looked out to discover where the security men were situated before Andy could once again force open the window. As it was on the other narrow side of the long building it was impossible to ascertain where the security men were placed. It was going to be a matter of pot luck and hope upon hope that they would be patrolling in another part of the mill.

Glen looked left and right out of the window and gave Andy the nod to start forcing the window at the old Victorian lock securing it. He once again placed the flat end of the crowbar in a narrow crevice near the handle of the window frame and jerked it violently to allow the window to swing inside just wide enough for the pair of them to climb out into the night air.

They waited to see if the security men were alerted by the creak of the window being forced open but there was no movement from that area. Glen climbed out first followed by Andy who handed the implements out to his nephew and allow him to leave without hindrance. He pushed the window back to a closed position and both glanced round the corner of the building to assess the best way of reaching the main gate at the far end of the courtyard.

This time luck was on their side as the security men had decided that another cup of tea was in order. The light from the hut and the music drifting out from it made Glen gauge that they had at least a small window of time to get out of this place before they were detected on the premises.

Their main problem now was passing by the security hut without being seen. Andy had been in similar tight spots many times before during his time overseas in the army. Without further ado he whispered instructions to his nephew.

'We'll move quietly across the courtyard until we just about reach the end of the hut,' he whispered. 'Push the crowbar into the gap under the hut, we can't take the chance of it falling out of your pocket and making a noise. Push it in as far as you can so that it can't be seen.'

'Then what?' asked Glen.

'We crawl across the length of the hut under the window on our stomachs until we get well past it,' he advised. 'And then we are off on our toes out of this place, pronto.'

There was no time to waste so they paced quietly across the courtyard and when they almost reached the end of the hut they slumped quietly down to the ground. The hut was raised off the ground on heavy breeze blocks to avoid damp rotting the timbers. Glen did as he was instructed namely pushing the crowbar silently as far under the hut as his arm could reach. He waited and watched as Andy crawled along the ground commando style on his elbows until he reached a point well past the door of the hut.

Glen followed suit and was pleased with himself how he was able to mimic what his uncle had exhibited beforehand. When he reached the point where Andy was crouching they quickly stood up before quietly moving over the courtyard and out of the main gate of the mill.

Once out of sight the pair sprinted down the street and hopped into the waiting Ford Anglia. Andy undertook a three point turn and the car sped towards the city centre and then onwards towards their local area before driving along the New Town Road. Once they would reach the McElroy residence the first thing to do would be a close examination of the incriminating documents that they had successfully seized from Benny Farr's secret hideout at the old mill.

CHAPTER EIGHTEEN
****

On the journey homeward Glen got to thinking about the methods his Uncle Andy had engaged in to break into the windows of the mill and disengage the locks on the doors as well as cracking the safe with what seemed a minimum of effort. In the past Andy was loath to talk about his time in the forces and Glen had never forced the issue. Thinking over events which took place in the past couple of hours he suspected that Andy may have been in some sort of special unit in the army.

Although he knew his uncle was not a voracious reader there was one book that sat on a bookshelf in the flat in Glasgow. The book told the story of Blair Mayne one of the founders of the Special Air Services in the Second World War and it seemed to take pride of place there but at the time Glen thought nothing of it. Until now! Maybe the truth of Andy's activities in the army might be revealed someday.

It was after midnight when they entered the house and both were surprised that Anna was still up and about. They suspected that she desired to see the pair of them home safely and she would want to know if Andy had been drinking and driving on their night out.

'Well, did you two have a good night out?' she asked.

'We had a brilliant time,' replied Andy winking at Glen.

'Where did you go?' Anna further asked.

'Oh! We were milling about on the other side of the city,' quipped Glen as he accentuated on the word milling.

'Not drinking too much I hope?' she once again asked a question mixed in with a demand.

'Not a drop,' replied Andy. 'In fact we had a different kind of night out.'

Andy looked at Glen waiting for the go-ahead to let Anna know the true nature of their excursion to the opposite side of the city. He motioned for his nephew to relate the story of their mission to the old mill on Shetland Close on the west side of Drumfast.

'Look Mum,' he started off, 'We have not been entirely truthful to you. When we said we had a different kind of night out that was true bill. We had to keep it from you why we were out tonight. The truth is we broke into an old spinning mill on the other side of town to get certain documentation that could ensure that I would never have to live in exile ever again.'

'How on earth could this so called documentation lead to you coming home for good?' asked Anna questioning the voracity of her son's last sweeping statement.

Glen pulled the A4 sheets out of the brown envelope and handed the document over to her. His mother scanned down the text her eyes opening ever wider as the name of her nephew Brian almost jumped out of page two on the sheet as well as the names, addresses and bank details of the leading members of the drug organisation on the first page. Anna handed the document back to Glen and sat in silence for a moment before staring intently at her son and brother sitting opposite her.

'You need to get rid of this document first thing in the morning,' she stated with a worried look on her face. 'This thing is too dangerous to have in your possession. It needs to go to the police so they can deal with it.'

'There's just one problem,' said Andy. 'Glen and I could be done for breaking and entering into the mill. I need to find some way of getting it to the local police area commander without divulging who I am.'

'Just post it,' advised Glen. 'If you stamp it first class it will get there next day.'

'That's the only way it can be done,' said Anna. 'I have stamps in the drawer in my bedroom. Throw it in the post box right away tonight and it will be collected first thing in the morning.'

Glen knew it would take at least a day for the police to organise raids over the area to arrest the overlords and foot soldiers of the drug cartel. He was supposed to report to Greg Bennet at The Liberty Arms the following evening to ensure that he would be leaving Drumfast once more to catch the train to Glasgow. However, Glen was determined to keep that appointment but with a twist.

Anna came down from her bedroom holding a sheet of first class stamps. Andy had written the address of the area police headquarters in capital letters to ensure that his handwriting could not be traced. In addition to the incriminating document he had written out a note, also in capital letters, indicating the location of the money in Benny Farr's office at the old mill. He closed the envelope and placed a row of sellotape across the flap to ensure added security in case the gum would come loose.

'Do you want to come with me Glen?' he asked. 'You probably know where the nearest post box is.'

'It's just outside the convenience store,' advised Glen as he placed on his jacket and the two of them jumped into the Ford Anglia. When they reached the post box Andy handed the envelope in a ceremonious fashion to Glen to allow him to post it and hopefully it would be the key for a welcome homecoming from his exile in Glasgow.

When they got home Anna had a cup of tea ready for them.

'Glen there is no need for you to meet Bennet and McGaughey later in the evening,' she asserted. 'Once this document gets into the hands of the police they and their gang will be dead meat.'

'Mum we need to lull those two and Brian into a sense of false security,' Glen replied. 'They need to think that the document is still in place at the mill. I also made a promise to Dad that I would get even with them and this evidence is one part of it.'

'What do you mean?' asked the increasingly worried Anna. 'What promise?'

Andy put his arm around his sister's shoulder and spoke in an assured tone. 'Anna the lad is correct. We need to make them unaware what is in store for them and Glen has unfinished personal business with them.'

'Andy I'm worried he is going to get himself hurt if he tackles them down at The Liberty Arms,' she cried.

'Mum I won't be starting anything in there,' he said. 'Uncle Andy will supposedly drive me to the station but take it from me I will not be catching any train to Glasgow. Now get yourself to bed, you look whacked out.'

Anna took her son's advice and slowly climbed the stairs hoping in her heart of hearts that her brother and son would stay safe over the coming days. She lay awake for some time until tiredness overcame her and she drifted into a deep sleep.

Downstairs Glen outlined what he required Andy to do the following evening. Instead of Bennet organising a taxi to take Glen to the railway station his uncle would wait outside The Liberty Arms in the Ford Anglia to give him a lift to the station. However, Glen had no intention of completing that journey as he had the unfinished business to undertake in the side streets off the New Town Road.

Glen, his mother and uncle spent the next day indoors listening to the radio. After enjoying the Jinky Jenkinson Show they hoped there would be no mention of any police raids on the drug organisation in the area during the news bulletin. Andy was convinced that it would take time for the law enforcement to coordinate a swoop, so no news was good news. Indeed the newscast was a mish-mash of political stories and the latest tales of woe from the manager of Drumfast United claiming that injuries to key players was the reason for their drop down the league table. Glen smiled to himself, some things never changed.

It was a matter of waiting until evening when it would be time for Glen to leave the house and travel to the New Town Road to report to Greg Bennet and Eddie McGaughey in The Liberty Arms. He knew he would have to stay cool and act subservient to these thugs until the time came later on to wreak his revenge and make good the promise he had made to his father Derek on his deathbed.

CHAPTER NINETEEN
****

As daylight faded and darkness descended over the Drumfast area Glen packed some items of clothing into the small travelling case he had brought with him from Glasgow. It was vital that Bennet and McGaughey were given the impression that he was leaving Drumfast for good that very evening so he decided to bring it into the bar to make his supposed exit from the city more believable.

'I'll see you later Mum,' he said as he kissed her on the cheek. 'Don't you worry, Andy and I will be back later on.'

'Just be very careful Glen,' Anna replied. 'These men are ruthless.'

'They won't be ruthless for much longer,' he said and after giving his mother a hug he sprinted down the garden path and jumped into the waiting Ford Anglia. When the motor glided close to the footpath outside The Liberty Arms Glen's uncle had one last word of advice before his nephew entered the bar.

'Stay calm no matter what they throw at you,' advised Andy. 'Just think of the bigger picture that'll be taking place over the next day or so. If you're not out of there within fifteen minutes I'm coming in to get you should I have to wreck the bar to get you out of there in one piece..'

Glen nodded in agreement but when he entered the crowded bar trailing his small suitcase behind him his uncle's advice was quickly forgotten when he viewed cousin Brian and his friend Jordy smirking over at him. He left the suitcase at the bar counter and pushed his way through the tables and issued a warning to his alarmed cousin.

'Someday that smile is going to be wiped off your face,' he seethed. 'Just keep looking over your shoulder because sooner or later you are going to get what's coming to you.'

Brian's mate Jordy rose to his feet. 'Do you want me to sort him out Brian?' he asked pulling his shoulders back ready for action. Brian said nothing. He just kept staring upwards at Glen towering above him.

Glen turned his attention to Jordy. 'You had better sit down right now because if you don't I'm going to knock you right through the back of that chair. The only thing you can sort out is the packets of Corn Flakes on the shelves of that supermarket you work in.'

Before Glen could hand out any form of retribution he felt a firm hand on his shoulder which succeeded in guiding him away from the scene of potential violence. Barney had been watching the situation unfolding and quickly moved out from behind the bar counter to ensure his young friend did not draw undue attention to himself.

'Listen son,' he quietly advised. 'Think of what is going to happen very soon. All this could be over in a matter of days if you stay cool and let things take their course.'

The patrons sitting around the scene of the interaction breathed a collective sigh of relief as the threat of tables and chairs being thrown or overturned had been avoided by the calming influence of the veteran bartender.

However, Glen was still seething as he collected the small suitcase and walked over to the office. He didn't bother to knock just pulling the door handle down and pushed it wide open with his left foot causing it to bang against the inside wall. Bennet and McGaughey looked up in surprise at this unexpected entrance which had disturbed their drinking session. On the desk was two tumblers and a half consumed litre bottle of whiskey which, by the look of the pair, had been completely full half an hour before.

'Did your parents not teach you any manners about knocking before you enter anybody's door,' Bennet slurred, well on his way to complete inebriation. Eddie McGaughey was not too far behind in these stakes.

'I only knock where I feel I'm going to be made welcome,' said Glen.

'Well, it goes without saying you're not welcome here. I don't want to see your face about this place for as long as I rule the roost around here,' Bennet boasted.

'Don't worry Greg, the next time you'll see my face it will be looking down at you and that goes for your fat friend here,' Glen was starting to get warmed up completely forgetting the two pieces of advice he had been given by his Uncle Andy and Barney the barman.

McGaughey was ready to answer the insult that Glen had thrown at him. He jumped up from his chair ready, in his own drunken mind, to give this young upstart a good hiding. However, he was stopped in his tracks by the commanding voice of his boss.

'Sit down Eddie,' said Bennet. 'This young scamp is not worth it. The bar is packed and I don't want the cops snooping around here if there is any trouble. The bar and entertainment license is up for renewal in three weeks time and we were lucky to get it last time.'

Glen was happy that he had said his piece although he was ready to have it out with the pair of them there and then but Bennet's attempt to cool things down had avoided that scenario. He glared at Glen who stared straight back.

'Just get out of here and think yourself lucky I don't have your kneecaps for castanets,' threatened Bennet.

'And remember what happened to the last young twat who spoke to Greg like that,' added Eddie McGaughey. 'He went through the back window and ended up in a wheelchair.'

Glen moved to the door and could not resist once last riposte. 'I'm shaking like a leaf,' he laughed and slammed the office door shut.

Barney leaned over the bar counter and issued one last word of advice. 'Move quickly lad before they decide to come after you along with Brian and that Jordy fellow. You were always an irritation to them but even more so now. Do what you have to do well away from here.'

'Will do Barney,' Glen replied and walked quickly out of the bar trailing his suitcase behind him.

'Thank goodness to see you in one piece,' remarked Andy as Glen hopped into the Ford Anglia. 'I was nearly ready to go in to get you out of there before the plan got blown out of the water.'

'No everything was cool,' Glen lied. 'We all just put our cards on the table so they are none the wiser what is going to happen in the next day or so.'

Andy slipped the gear stick into first and the car moved off along the New Town Road towards the location of the train station. Near to the periphery of the main thoroughfare Andy pulled the vehicle into a side street well away from any prying eyes which could be scanning their movements along the road from the entrance of The Liberty Arms.

His uncle was worried regarding Glen's further intentions that evening. In his opinion the forces of law and order would be adequate to ensure that revenge would fall on the heads of the people who had made the McElroy family's life a misery over the past three years. However, he knew there was no point in persuading his nephew to desist from taking the avenue of personal revenge that evening.

'We need to wait here until it is almost closing time at the bar,' he advised his uncle. 'Are you ok to wait here?'

'Of course I am,' replied Andy. 'I have come so far in this venture with you and there is no way I'm backing out now. Is there no way I could even come with you to help finish this off? The two of us would make quick work of these two.'

'No!' stated Glen adamantly. 'If this goes belly up I need you to be kept well out of this part in case my Mum needs your support.'

'If you say so. But one piece of advice if you have to wait about be patient and for goodness sake stay cool until Bennet comes close to you,' replied Andy as the pair sat in silence waiting for the hours to tick by. When it was time for Glen to leave he shook hands with his uncle and sprinted along the back streets of the New Town Road until he could view The Liberty Arms from an alleyway in the street opposite.

As he waited for closing time at the bar he leaned against the alley wall and questioned himself if this was the correct way to wreak revenge to help remove the hurt and stress of the past three years. Just as a huge doubt was starting to overcome his mind he remembered the words his father had spoken to him on the evening before he died. *'The situation we are in now will require drastic action, namely to avenge what has been done to you personally and which has affected this family as well. You will need to find some way of returning to Drumfast for good.'* That thought was enough for him to continue on the path he was about to take in the coming hour.

His innermost thoughts were disturbed by the sound of laughter coming from across the road as two men exited The Liberty Arms followed by another two younger men in a similar drunken state linking arms with two girls. The two young men were Brian Wharton and his pal Jordy. A taxi drew up and they bundled the women into the back of the cab and then waved at the two older men out of an open widow at the rear door of the vehicle.

Greg Bennet and Eddie McGaughey stood talking for a minute before Bennet staggered across the New Town Road towards the street where Glen had hidden himself. McGaughey fell about laughing as his associate almost fell foul of a passing car which had to brake suddenly just inches from him. Glen could hear insults being hurled from both directions as Bennet stood in front of the vehicle banging his fist on the bonnet. The startled driver immediately reversed, swerved around the angry pedestrian and accelerated at speed out of a potential dangerous altercation. Bennet shook his fist at the retreating car, shouted a few choice drunken words and then proceeded to make his unsteady way into the street staggering step by step towards the alleyway.

This was the night of the long knives when chickens would come home to roost. Glen was determined to have his personal revenge on the three people who had been the leading players in the forced exile from his home city and the people he loved. As the footsteps came ever closer Glen was tempted to jump out and confront Bennet in the street but Andy had advised him to think coolly so he waited until his enemy was just about to pass his alleyway hiding place.

'Psst mate,' Glen's disguised voice floated out from the alley. 'Got any gear on you?' He then gave out a muffled cough as if he was in some sort of pain.

Bennet stopped dead when the voice with a husky tone addressed him from the depths in the alleyway. He peered into the darkness and was curious to discover who was speaking to him and was requesting a supply of narcotics. Anger was welling up in him at the thought of some junkie requesting a deal from him personally. He didn't lower himself at this stage of the operation to deal directly with the punters, leaving that end of the business to the lower orders such as Brian Wharton.

'If I find out who you are, you are going to be sorry you spoke to me thinking I would be carrying anything on me in the open,' he shouted and proceeded to enter the alleyway. 'Who are you anyway?' he barked out once again.

'Oh! I'm somebody who has business with you but it's not the dirty line of business you deal in,' said Glen who had waited until Bennet had come close enough to allow him to get a firm grip on the lapels of his enemy's jacket.

Once within range he landed two swift blows to side of Bennet's face knocking him to the floor of the alleyway where he landed with a thud with his back against the brick wall. As his nemesis attempted to rise up to defend himself Glen landed other right hander to the jaw rendering Bennet semi-conscious. Glen's knuckles were starting to hurt so he decided to leave part one of his revenge mission lying against the alley wall.

'Do you remember me saying the next time you will see my face it would be staring down at you. Well, have a good look.' Glen sneered. 'These three punches are for each year I have had to live in exile and this one is for the threatening letter you posted through our letterbox on the night of my dad's funeral.'

Bennet looked up hoping that the punishment Glen was meting out would end and end soon. But it wasn't over. He gave Bennet a final goodbye with a kick into his stomach and then in the form of a left hander to the other side of his jaw this time wishing to save his right hand for the next stage of the operation. Glen left Bennet propped up against the wall feeling no pity whatsoever for the man who had heaped misery on himself and his family over the past three years.

Eddie McGaughey lived on his own two streets way from Bennet. His wife had left him three years before refusing to stay in a marriage whereby she was allowed next to nothing in possessions and more importantly the right to enjoy personal freedom. Meanwhile her spouse enjoyed all the benefits of a single man as he drank with his friend Greg Bennet every night in The Liberty Arms and showed scant respect for her rolling home most nights in the early hours of the morning. The poor woman had enough and one night took off to live with her sister in Canada in an attempt to carve out another life well out of the clutches of the abusive Eddie McGaughey.

As Glen raced onwards towards the street where Bennet's second in command lived, the thought struck him that he didn't really know the exact number of the house where McGaughey lived. Luckily at this late hour only one light was showing in the window and another in the hallway at the front of the residence. He reckoned that Eddie had arrived home and possibly proceeded to make himself a cup of coffee or tea and something to eat before retiring to bed.

Glen rang the doorbell and waited patiently for the ring tone to be answered. After what seemed to be an interminably long time he could hear the bolts in the inside door being opened and the outside door slowly creaked opened just enough for the occupant to peep out to see who was calling at this late hour. McGaughey's eyes almost popped out of his head when the person he viewed standing outside was the very one who was supposed to be on the night train to Glasgow.

'Good evening Eddie, I'm sure you're surprised to see me standing out here at this late hour,' said Glen in a somewhat quiet manner. 'Are you not going to invite me in?'

MvGaughey made a movement to close the door in Glen's face but the young man had preempted this action and kicked the door with the full force of his size nine boot in roughhouse fashion which flung it open wide. It knocked the occupant on the other side through the open security door on the other side of the small hallway and sent him sprawling on the flat of his back as the door caught him full force on the front of his body.

Glen didn't wait for a formal invitation from his one time torturer. He slammed the front door shut to avoid wakening up the neighbourhood and quickly got to work on taking revenge on his number two enemy. Without Greg Bennet by his side McGaughey was not the tough guy that he projected towards the young men who worked for the organisation. As he lay on the ground defenceless all Glen could do was give McGaughey a couple of blows with his left fist as the man attempted to sit up. His right hand was aching due to the punishment he had meted out to Bennet in the alleyway.

At last Eddie McGaughey spoke. 'Wait until Greg hears about this,' he moaned. 'You'll be exiled all right, but it will be in a box.'

'Is that so?' replied Glen who could feel the anger welling up inside him once again. 'Only if he can get the strength to get home from the alleyway where I left him propped up against the wall.'

'You think living in Glasgow has made you into some sort of tough guy,' shouted McGaughey as he shakily made to get up and take issue with his attacker. Glen allowed him to get to his feet and he stood face to face with the man who was one of the instigators of forcing him to live away from his family for such a long time.

'I learned a lot of things living in Glasgow, some good and some bad,' said Glen. 'When somebody like you puts their face almost up against your face you give them what is called a Glasgow kiss. Here's an example of it!'

As McGaughey attempted to move out of the way Glen grabbed him by the lapels of his coat and head butted him straight on the nose. With blood spurting out of his nostrils McGaughey fell once again to the ground clutching his face and yelling in pain.

'Hopefully this will be the last time I'll be forced to be in your company or in the company of that rat Bennet,' said Glen as he moved towards the door knowing that his night's work had been completed. 'Have a great life Eddie. Hopefully it will be staring at the walls of a prison cell where you belong.'

In his opinion the actions taken this evening were unavoidable. The debt of honour to his father had almost been paid in full. The only person who had not felt the full force of his revenge was his cousin Brian Wharton who had started the chain of events leading to the exile from his home city.

There had been enough violence perpetrated this evening. The knuckles in his hands were aching and his forehead throbbed so he decided that the long arm of the law would be sufficient to inflict punishment on his snake of a relative who would be unaware what was waiting for him the next morning.

CHAPTER TWENTY
****

It only took a matter of eight minutes for Glen to wind his way through the streets which led to the other end of the New Town Road. He reached the Ford Anglia which was still parked in the same spot and a relieved Uncle Andy started the engine and proceeded to drive the car in the opposite direction towards home.

'I was going to give you another couple of minutes,' Andy said. 'I was hoping you hadn't bitten off more that you could chew.'

'They were not expecting me to return so I had the element of surprise,' replied Glen. 'They'll never catch on that the police have the document so both of them will think that this was just a revenge attack before I left for Glasgow.'

'We will have to get back quickly in case they send some of their cronies to the house,' advised Andy. 'I just hope the law gets to the lot of them before they can organise any reprisals.'

As the Ford Anglia pulled up outside the house a worried Anna opened the door and stood glancing up and down the street as her son and brother walked briskly up the path. They entered the hallway and moved into the living room where Glen slumped down satisfied that his night's exertions had been a success.

As usual Anna rushed to the kitchen to put the kettle on for a welcome cup of tea. Andy looked at Glen's hands and noticed that they were starting to swell and would eventually discolour. He immediately went to the kitchen and pulled out a couple of frozen packets of peas from the freezer. Anna looked at him quizzically but soon realised the reason for her brother's raid on the freezer when he pointed to his knuckles.

'Hold one of these over the knuckles on your right hand,' he commanded Glen. 'Your left one isn't quite so bad so I'll hold this other one on to your forehead in case it swells up.'

Anna came in holding a tray containing three cups and a plate of sandwiches. She looked with alarm at Glen holding the frozen peas over his right hand and Andy pressing the other packet on his nephew's forehead.

'Glen I hope you think this was worth it, especially as the police will soon be swinging into action to get these people,' she said.

'Make no mistake about it mother, it was worth it,' he replied. 'I hope Dad is looking down and smiling down at us, for that was one of his last requests to me.'

'Well, I hope this is the end of the violence. Let's drink this cup of tea and get up to bed,' she said and left it there.

All three eventually trooped up the stairs but Andy decided to keep watch from his bedroom window in case Bennet sent some of his cohorts to attack the house. As dawn broke it was evident that there was no reprisal forthcoming from that quarter. Little did the occupants of the McElroy household know that as daylight was lighting up the Drumfast area the police operation against the drugs organisation had swung into swift action.

After becoming fully conscious after the beating Glen had given him Bennet struggled home and was washing the blood away from his face in preparation to lie down and rest for a couple of hours. He lay on the bed with revenge on his mind wondering if his attacker was still in the area or had indeed taken the train to Glasgow. He would make preparations in the morning to sort Glen McElroy out whether he was still in Drumfast or back living in Glasgow.

As he drifted into an unsettled sleep, rolling from side to side on the bed, three police command vehicles moved quietly into the street in the early hours of the morning. The officers dismounted and waited for the signal from their commander to enter the property. Bennet was aroused by the crash of his front door caving in under the force of a small battering ram which the police call 'the big red key'. Before he could painfully drag himself out of bed the door of his room burst open and he was immediately surrounded by six officers in combat uniform.

The tall and imposing senior officer stood at the end of the bed and read out the charge that Bennet would be arrested under. 'Gregory Bennet you are hereby arrested under Section 5a of the Supply of Drugs Act 1997 relating to the Supply and Production of Controlled Substances. Anything you say can be used against you in court. You have the right to remain silent. Anything you say can and will be used against you in a court of law. You have the right to an attorney. If you cannot afford an attorney, one will be provided for you.'

The officer stared at the stunned man and added, 'By the way what happened to your face?'

'I was assaulted by a bloke called Glen McElroy on my way home from my business at The Liberty Arms on the New Town Road. It was an unprovoked attack and I want him arrested,' Bennet replied.

'Well that would be your word against his. Now get dressed and we'll get on our way to the station where you can get in contact with your brief,' said the officer who asked. 'By the way who is your solicitor?'

'It is Benny Farr,' replied Bennet.

'Mm! That could be a problem,' said the officer. 'Benjamin Farr was arrested earlier this morning on a charge of possessing the proceeds of crime in addition to money laundering on a large scale in tax havens in England and the continent of Europe . I think you may need a duty solicitor'

'I know nothing about that,' said Bennet. 'You can search my house here and my office in The Liberty Arms. You will find nothing here and over there to prove that I have anything to do with this charge.'

'Well we can discuss this further down at the station,' the officer replied. 'Just get dressed and we will get on our way when my men have finished searching your house.'

After around half an hour a sergeant popped his head around the door and informed the senior officer that the premises were as clean as a whistle.

'I told you so,' said Bennet with a smirk on his face. 'Is there any point in taking me in.'

'Don't you worry about that,' replied the officer. 'We have enough information on a document we have received to bang you to rights plus there is no doubt that one or other of your compatriots will eventually give us all we need. Right, hurry up we need to get going. I don't want the people living in this street alarmed at what is going on here.'

A crestfallen Bennet got hastily dressed and was led out to the police vehicle with curtains being twitched as the householders watched their neighbour being escorted with his hands handcuffed behind his back. Most were hoping that this would be the last they will see of the notorious Greg Bennet.

An identical operation was taking place two streets away where Eddie McGaughey was pleading his innocence and threatening to take legal action against Glen McElroy. The arresting officer had no interest in his protestations and he was similarly handcuffed and led into a police vehicle to be taken to the interview suite at the police station.

Bennet and McGaughey were placed in separate interview rooms and intensive interrogations proceeded with both loudly voicing their innocence at first to the charges. Each were given a duty solicitor as Benny Farr was in the similar situation as themselves. As each question was put to them the only answer was a 'no comment'.

After a series of stalemates the interviewing officer suddenly pulled out of a binder the document that Andy had posted anonymously the few evenings previously He pushed it in front of Bennet who stared intently at it before answering negatively.

'I know nothing about this,' he said arrogantly. 'You will find that this was not in my possession here or in The Liberty Arms.'

'Oh we know that,' replied the experienced interviewing officer. 'We received this over the post from an unknown source together with an address on the north side of the city. Our colleagues from that area have raided an office belonging to a bogus company called Benfar Associates Limited and when we ordered the rental papers relating to this firm we found this was the office of none other than a Mr. Benny Farr. This is why you needed a duty solicitor. He is now in custody and hopefully will soon be singing like a canary.'

'I know nothing about this paper,' protested Bennet. 'This is a fit up by the heads of this drug organisation.'

'Come off it Greg,' laughed the interviewing officer. 'This is the type of info we have been waiting to get for the past ten years. Your dabs are all over it. This was your insurance policy in case the top guys decided to dispense with your services.'

Once again Greg Bennet resumed his no comment position but the police now had enough to finally charge him and McGaughey with peddling drugs and money laundering. As he sat in silence his mind was mulling over the various avenues he could take to negotiate a lighter sentence if he could turn state evidence and go into a witness protection programme.

The document was useless now to ensure his safety from the leaders of the cartel so the witness protection programme seemed to be the best way to ensure a lighter sentence when he would be up in court. McGaughey could paddle his own canoe and negotiate whatever he wished to do with the law. It was every man for himself now and he had absolutely no interest what would happen to his number two when the law took its course.

'It looks like you have me bang to rights,' he finally said to the interviewing officer after a quick conversation with the duty solicitor. 'There is a lot more I can tell you that is not in that document. You need to give me a way out of a heavy sentence as my life will not be worth living after today.'

'I'll have to talk to my superiors but from previous experience in this field you could get off with a lighter sentence, but that would be up to the judge. It's down to you to give us everything you know,' the officer advised.

With the information on the document and Greg Bennet adding plenty more significant information the raids all over the city gave the police a goldmine of evidence as the doors of Benny Farr and the leading members of the cartel had been smashed down in an organised operation by the drugs squads. The head men of the organisation were angry and perplexed as they were led away to various police stations wondering how the long arm of the law had reached them. Little did they know that one of their own had helped bring about their downfall by his own devious means.

Later in the morning as Brian Wharton strolled out of his house he was unaware that the police were waiting to pounce hoping that he had narcotics on his person ready to sell that morning. As he was only a member of the lower ranks in the organisation the police did not see fit to place vehicles to surround his house and break down the door. In his case a small covert operation would suffice.

Brian was in a good mood thinking his cousin Glen McElroy was far away in Glasgow and out of his life for ever. He was now able to go about his business of peddling drugs in the neighbourhood without having to look over his shoulder for any reprisal coming his way. Just as he was passing an alleyway a voice spoke quietly from within the opening. 'Psst mate! Got any gear for sale?'

Wharton peered into the alleyway to see a tall thin figure dressed in a light grey jacket with a hood covering most of his face which was usually the normal dress code for someone hoping to score drugs. Greed overtook caution and Wharton stepped into the alley and replied to the man's request.

'Show me your money first,' he said as he pulled some small packets of cocaine out of his jacket pocket. 'All I have with me are some wraps of coke at the moment.'

The man pulled four twenty pound notes out of his pocket which was enough to purchase two grams of the narcotic. The two exchanged the money and the drugs and each placed the items of the deal into their pockets. Brian Wharton was elated that he had started the day with enough cash in his person to pay Greg Bennet and still have enough to see him through the rest of the day. Any other deals would be icing on the cake.

'I'll need to score regularly,' the other man said his hand shaking visibly. 'Probably every day if this gets worse.'

'Well, there's plenty more where this came from,' laughed Wharton. 'I can meet you here around this time tomorrow if you like.'

He made a move to leave the alley but suddenly three burly men dressed in various types of jackets appeared at the narrow opening. With no warning the purchaser of the cocaine grabbed him by the shoulders, turned him around and pushed his face against the brick wall of the alleyway. Wharton was starting to panic thinking that this was a robbery by rival team from another part of the city. When the purchaser spoke his worst fears were starting to be realised.

The other men entered the alley and started to frisk Wharton pulling a wad of money out of one pocket and six wraps of cocaine from his inside jacket.

'Brian Wharton I am arresting you for the possession and supplying of a Class A Drug namely cocaine under the Misuse of Drugs Act 1975. Anything you say can be used against you in court. You have the right to remain silent. Anything you say can and will be used against you in a court of law. You have the right to an attorney. If you cannot afford an attorney, one will be provided for you.'

'This is entrapment,' yelled Wharton. 'There is no way you can prove this. Your dabs will be all over the wraps as well as mine.'

'Do you think we are stupid and we came up the river in a bubble,' the officer laughed as he held up his hand which was covered in a thin flesh coloured rubber glove. 'The only fingerprints on these wraps will be yours.'

'This is still entrapment,' protested Wharton.

'We use any means at our disposal to get vermin like you off the streets,' the police sergeant said and then added. 'In the words of a recent hit record *it's a rat trap and you've been caught.*'

The other officers laughed heartily and led Brian Wharton out of the alley and into the waiting police car. Although it had taken a long time it looked like what goes round comes around and in his case Wharton would get what he deserved for his devious past actions.

CHAPTER TWENTY ONE
****

Still unaware of all the police activities which had been taking place over the city Anna, Glen and Andy each readied themselves the following morning and came downstairs to have breakfast at the kitchen table.

'Put the radio on Anna,' requested Andy who was extremely anxious to hear if anything had been reported about the two assaults on Bennet and McGaughey the previous evening.

To their surprise the announcer said that they were going straight over to Drumfast Police Headquarters for an important announcement. The three listened intently as the confident voice of a police spokesman came over the airwaves.

'This morning the Tactical Drugs Unit of the Drumfast Police Service undertook a number of raids in various parts of the city. Information had recently come into our hands regarding leading members of an organisation which has been operating in the narcotics sphere all over the city. A number of men have been apprehended and are now in police custody where they are being interviewed by officers in various police stations in the city.'

'Who are these people?' a television reporter spoke up before the officer could continue.

'We cannot divulge any names until they are formally charged,' replied the spokesman, 'but rest assured when they are charged the names of these men will be released to the local media. That is all I can say in the meantime. Thank you for your attendance here this morning.'

Glen looked at his mother and uncle and a big smile broke out over his face. Although his fists were still aching from the previous night the pain paled into insignificance with the news of the arrests. How he wished he was a fly on the wall to enable him to listen to the interviews at the police station where Bennet and McGaughey and his cousin were being held.

When they were just about to finish breakfast a loud knock came to the door and when Andy answered the door his sister Sarah pushed past him in an agitated and distressed state.

Knowing she would get little words of comfort from her nephew and brother she addressed herself directly to her sister. Glen and Andy stood back and waited to hear any information regarding Sarah's errant son Brian.

'Anna, my Brian has been arrested this morning and he is in a police station,' she cried. 'There is supposed to be a charge of dealing drugs. It must be a trumped up charge. He would never do anything like this.'

'Now you know how I felt,' interjected Glen with a broad grin on his face.

Anna was the type of lady who went out of her way to avoid confrontation but she felt she had to say something that needed to be stated over the past number of years.

'Sarah, were you so blind that you could not see what was going on before your very eyes,' she started off. 'How do you think Brian was making a living all this time?'

'He was working for Greg Bennet helping out in The Liberty Arms,' she replied. 'Greg and Eddie have been very good to him.'

'Just as long as he peddled enough drugs to give them a comfortable living,' said Andy. 'He was one of their top salesmen.'

'Let's be truthful Sarah,' added Anna. 'He has ruined your life now as well as that of young Marlene. I think she realised long ago the big mistake she made marrying him.'

Sarah made to leave the room as there was no encouragement or succour coming from the people there But not before she fired a last salvo as she left the house.

'I will never believe my son has been mixed up in drug dealing.' she shouted. 'It's funny all this trouble has blown up since you two arrived back from Glasgow. You, Glen, have always been jealous of my Brian's success and his marriage to Marlene.'

'His success! Jealous of a drug dealer, never,' Glen laughed. 'I just wished I had taken the chance to get to him before the police snatched him.'

'That's all you know, violence,' she retorted.

'Better than peddling death to kids on the streets,' added Andy. 'Hope they stick him away for a long time.'

Sarah left the house almost taking the hinges off the door as she slammed it shut in anger at Andy's last remark.

'It looks like he'll have to murder somebody before she will wise up,' said Anna.

'With the stuff he peddles around the place he probably could have done that already,' replied Andy.

Glen decided to lighten things up and went into the kitchen to turn on the radio once again. He opened the door which led into the back garden and listened as the music from the Jinky Jenkinson show drifted across the room. When the song ended the voice of their good friend intimated that he would be signing off in a couple of moments.

'Just before I go and we head into the midday news I would like to dedicate the final song today to friends of mine namely the McElroy family. These people have had a really rough time over the past number of years and hopefully there are better times ahead for them. This tune is taken off a new album recorded live at the recent Drumfast Song.Contest. Here is 'This Land Is Not A Home' and was written by the late Derek McElroy who was an old pal of mine. With that I bid you good bye and wish you a happy and peaceful day.'

Glen reached over and turned the radio to its maximum volume as the voices of the gospel choir echoed around the house. Anna and Andy rushed into the kitchen to find Glen staring out into the garden with tears in his eyes. They stood behind him not wishing to disturb his thoughts but as the music continued he motioned them to join him and they proceeded to link arms in a tribute to their beloved dead relative.

When the song ended and the music heralding the start of the news bulletin came over the airwaves Glen walked over and turned the radio off. He once again moved over to the back door and to the surprise of his mother and uncle he voiced a tribute of his own to his father as he looked up to the sky.

'Dad, that song on Jinky's programme was for you. I hope you are looking down and smiling at us. At long last your talent has been recognised and you have left a lasting legacy for the three of us here. Thank you Dad!'

Three years of anguish seemed to disappear into the air as Glen and Andy sat down at the kitchen table while Anna, as usual, put the kettle on for a welcome cup of tea. When the dust of the previous couple of weeks would settle down Andy decided he could return to Glasgow to start work once again and resume his lifestyle in that city. Glen and Anna intimated that they would accompany him to bring Glen's belongings back to Drumfast. This time for good.

Anna felt a sense of pity for her sister Sarah. Perhaps she might come to believe the nefarious activities her son Brian had been up to when the court cases would start later in the year. She sat in silent contemplation as Glen slipped the compact disc of the contest tunes into the radio/player. He chose song number two and the sound of Derek's song once again drifted over the kitchen bringing a smile to all three faces.

This was Derek's last song and the words of the first line he had written down were a fitting epitaph to his memory. 'This land is not a home til everyone is free.' With the likes of Greg Bennet and Eddie McGaughey heading for a long jail term his son was now able to live his life free from the threat of exile, violence and suspicion.

Andy's eventful two-week holiday sadly came to an end and the family left the city by train after taking the Ford Anglia back to the rental company. Glen's uncle would miss his nephew and the flat would seem empty when his belongings headed back to Drumfast. However, his mother needed him more so it was all for the better. Andy knew if he was needed in a family emergency it was only a train journey away from the city of his birth.

As far as a relationship with Marlene was concerned, Glen had mixed feelings on that score. He had developed a sense of pity for her since he had escorted her to the phone box on the night of his father's death. As far as any serious romantic developments which may or may not take place in the future that was entirely up to her in his mind. If she decided to divorce Brian that could be a possibility but at the moment his main priority was to support his mother in the first throes of widowhood.

He also needed to forge a new life in Drumfast with the hope that he could resume his career as a compositor in the printing works where he once worked. If Marlene and himself resumed as a couple that was something that needed to be put on the long finger until things settled down over the ensuing months or even in a year or two.

The previous three years in exile and the missed time with his family could never be recovered but the next period had the possibility to be a time of peace and happiness for Glen, Anna and the extended McElroy family. A time when the black cloud which had hovered over their lives would disappear and the sunny blue skies would once again look down on the household as they attempt to honour the memory of Derek McElroy and the song he had left them as his final legacy.

THE END

Printed in Great Britain
by Amazon